Praise for
SID HITE'S
Stick and Whittle

S0-AYT-660

"Hite crafts a friendship-adventure story that is both lighthearted and deep with likeable, well-rounded characters. . . . Hite spins a yarn with enough adventure to please action fans, while the strength of the title characters makes it richer than a typical buddy story."   —*VOYA*

"Hite packs a saddlebag full of timeless plot elements, from an exquisitely crafted rescue to the satisfying fruition of love at first sight, and freshens these tried and true devices with dead-on pacing and a strong sense of place . . . a credit to the genre."   —*BCCB*

"Seasoned with the same tall-tale flavor as the author's Dithers books, this tongue-in-cheek post-Civil War novel combines rip-roaring adventure with Hite's familiar themes of unrequited love, enduring friendship, and the mysterious power of fate. . . . Hite's off-beat western is sure to draw new fans as they relish the book's dry humor, colorful language, and passel or surprises."   —*Publishers Weekly*

"This lighthearted western satisfies . . . a treasure for this audience."
— *School Library Journal*

A *Smithsonian* Notable Book

A New York Public Library Title for Reading and Sharing

STICK & WHITTLE

BY
Sid Hite

SCHOLASTIC INC.
New York Toronto London Auckland Sydney
Mexico City New Delhi Hong Kong Buenos Aires

STICK AND WHITTLE IS AN
ADVENTURE NOVEL SET IN A
HISTORICAL TIME. ALTHOUGH
EVERY ATTEMPT HAS BEEN MADE
TO ACCURATELY DEPICT THE TIME
AND PLACE OF THIS STORY, IT
IS INTENDED TO ENTERTAIN
AND DOES NOT STRIVE TO BE A
FACTUAL HISTORICAL NOVEL.

— SID HITE

ONE

MELVIN FITCHETT WAS feeling pretty good about life as the orange ball of the sun began its daily descent over the Great Staked Plains of north Texas. He'd not seen another person nor slept under a roof during the past three days or nights, but he didn't care. Socializing and comfort were not high on Melvin's agenda. Independence was the important thing. He had recently quit a job he'd held for the past four years and was happy just to be moving on.

Although Melvin was feeling footloose and free, the same could not be said for his beast of burden, Mercy. Unlike Melvin, she still had her job, and the vast, treeless plain they were crossing was hard on a horse. All the same, she plodded along without complaint. Melvin had always been good to her. She thought he was a god.

Melvin could tell by the way the land was changing character that the Red River lay somewhere in the near distance. Drawing him forward was a vaguely remembered fishing hole. It had been several years since he'd passed this way and fished the hole, but if his memory served correctly, it sat in the crooked arm of a sandy peninsula protruding from the north bank of the river. The bank stood taller than a man and was lined with windblown cottonwoods that protected the lower ground. It was an ideal site for camping and Melvin was hoping luck would deliver him there before nightfall.

Melvin Fitchett believed in luck, for better or worse. As far as he was concerned, luck was the most important force in the universe. It was the reason he was alive. Mention luck to Melvin and his eyes glazed with mystical notions. Otherwise, generally, he was a practical man.

The month was June, the year, 1872, and as the growing darkness shrank the plains around them, Melvin and Mercy were some ninety miles north of Fort Worth, Texas, approximately fifteen miles west of the Chisholm Trail. By most accounts, they were in Comanche territory, although an Apache fighter might have argued the fact and a United States Army officer would have also contested the claim. The officer would insist that the Red River ran through the state of Texas and all Indians in the area were off their assigned reservations. He would likely add that said Indians were hostile renegades and warn you to guard against your life. Hmph. So much for the kind advice of army officers. If you were dumb enough not to know that a roving Comanche was a threat to your physical well-being, then you were excessively stupid and ought never to have been traveling alone in north Texas. Not in 1872.

If Melvin had his druthers, he would not be discussing territorial sovereignty with anyone. He wasn't looking for trouble. He just wanted to make his way north through the Indian Nations and proceed to Abilene, Kansas, where several years before he had deposited five hundred and fifty hard-earned dollars in a Wells Fargo bank. He wanted to collect his money, plus interest, and afterwards return east to the small farm in Virginia where he was raised. Or perhaps not. In the back of his mind he was always looking for the girl who had grown up on a neighboring farm and claimed his heart in childhood. Her name was Evelyn Laroue. He'd not seen her in eight long years, yet he had reason to believe she might be somewhere on the frontier . . . and if she was, all of his plans were subject to change. However, just now he was in north Texas where first things come first and his main objective was to reach the Kansas border in one piece.

Melvin and Mercy soon came to a low ridge lying horizontally across their path. As they ascended the elevated land a startled fox barked and scurried from a thicket of grass. Melvin and Mercy paused on the high ground. Mercy whinnied excitedly. Moisture had tickled her nostrils and she knew water was near. Melvin sighed contentedly. Down below was the Red River. At this time of year and this far west, it was little more than a fair-sized stream. Still, it was there and it was wet, and as Melvin squinted into the twi-light he beheld a sandbar. Beyond it stood a string of weath-ered cottonwoods. Melvin was in luck. This was the spot he'd been seeking.

They descended the ridge, crossed the shallow river and halted on the peninsula beneath the branches of a cotton-wood. Melvin took the bridle from Mercy's mouth, removed her saddle, his rifle and his supply bags, then sent his thirsty mount to drink while he gathered fallen branches and bramble for a fire. As he collected the wood he tossed it toward a boulder sitting in the middle of the sandbar. Some-where in the back of his mind it occurred to him that he did not remember any boulders near the fishing hole, yet he did not stop what he was doing to ponder the matter. Melvin wanted to get settled before the night finished falling around him. Besides, he knew the sort of tricks time tended to play on his memory. He'd found the hole. That was good enough for him.

Although he had store-bought matches in his saddlebag, they were intended for emergency use, so he sparked a fire with flint on steel instead. Melvin stood back as a flame licked the tinder, waiting until he was sure the kindling caught, then turned to fetch a slab of salt-cured beef and a can of succotash from his packs. He placed the can by the fire, lay the beef on top of the air-tight vegetables and sat down to remove his boots. While he was rubbing his tired feet Mercy ambled up from the river and stood behind him.

"That's my girl," Melvin mumbled tenderly. "You be patient now. I'll serve your oats presently."

Mercy neighed and shifted her weight from haunch to haunch. The fire crackled. The river gurgled. Melvin yawned. He'd been traveling since early morning. His eyelids grew heavy and drooped . . . then flew abruptly open as the nearby boulder behaved in a very unrocklike manner. The confounded thing shot into the air, transformed from a solid mass into a fluttering sphere, split into separate forms and screamed, "Yeeoooww!"

Melvin was astounded, discombobulated, confused and perplexed all in the same instant. How could he fathom what his eyes were telling him? A short troll wearing a black derby had thrown aside a smoking blanket and now ran toward the river. The diminutive troll — or maybe it was a pygmy ragamuffin — dashed across the peninsula and plunged headlong into the water.

Melvin turned to Mercy, wondering if she saw the same apparition he was seeing. Evidently she did. Her ears were pressed flat against her head and her eyes were bigger around than silver dollars. Melvin gulped and redirected his stunned senses to where the unknown creature was thrashing.

Soon a dripping wet form emerged from the river, shook excess water from its extremities and started toward the fire. Melvin was flummoxed. Walking toward him was a skinny boy with stringy brown hair.

"Go ahead and shoot if you want," the boy said as he strode boldly forward. "But it wouldn't be proper. You've got me at an unfair disadvantage."

Melvin's jaw fell open. He gestured that he held no weapons and meant no harm.

The boy glared sternly at Melvin, his eyes warning him not to make any sudden moves. Then the boy plopped down by the fire and began to shed his wet boots, which were in pitiful condition and worn without socks. As the boy yanked off his second sad boot a small, single-shot pistol fell to the ground. He glanced at the derringer, glanced at Melvin, then rose nonchalantly to his feet and selected a sturdy stick from the pile of wood by the fire. He stuck the stick in the sand, removed his cotton jacket and hung it up to dry. Afterwards he took off his shirt and employed yet another stick in the same manner. The whole while Melvin's mouth was agape and his mind racing to make peace with reality. The boy ran his fingers through his tangled hair, sat again by the fire and casually declared, "It's a good thing I know how to swim."

Melvin was mum.

The boy looked around, hesitated, then shook his head and lamented, "Durn. I lost my hat. I'll have to go find it in the morning. Hope the river doesn't carry it away."

Melvin nodded.

The boy shot a dubious look at his host. "Mister, I know you can talk. I heard you speaking to your horse."

Melvin swallowed and managed to whisper. "I, ah . . . thought you were a rock."

A proud grin spread over the youngster's face. He reached for the discarded blanket and declared, "Old Apache trick."

"Excuse me?"

The boy explained, "It's got to be a gray blanket, or maybe brown. Anyway, you cover it with moss and sand and stuff, and from a distance it looks like a rock."

"Oh."

The boy's grin suddenly sank into a frown. "Yeah . . . well, the trick was working just fine until you built a fire up against me."

"Sorry," Melvin mumbled sincerely. The kid looked as if he had been suffering an extended run of bad luck and Melvin felt genuinely remiss about adding to the youngster's woes.

Down on his luck or not, the boy's spirit had not been broken. "No need to apologize, Mister. I was fixing to ambush you."

Melvin's eyebrows arched upward.

The boy shook his head and said, "You're lucky though. There's a problem with the trick I just discovered. You can't see out from under the blanket after it gets dark."

Melvin could hardly believe what was happening. Here he was, sitting by the Red River in the middle of nowhere listening to a bedraggled lad discuss a tactical flaw in an ancient Apache ambush technique. It was, to say the least, an entirely unexpected development . . . which was still unfolding.

As Melvin watched, the boy picked up his derringer, pointed skyward and pulled the trigger. Except for the thwack of the hammer striking a wet powder cap, nothing happened. The gunman grimaced, casually dropped the weapon on the ground, leaned back on his elbows and observed, "That's a pretty mare you've got."

"Thank you. Her name is Mercy."

Slowly but surely, the boy's gaze moved from Melvin's face to the slab of beef sitting atop the can of succotash. Although he did not actually salivate, he apparently coveted the meat. "So, Mister, you fixing to eat?"

"I was," Melvin confirmed.

The boy tore his attention away from the beef and peered into the fire. Melvin could see the youngster was famished, and was about to offer him supper when the boy spoke first. "I'll be straight with you, Mister, I'm no scoundrel. I've got standards. I never cause trouble for anyone that feeds me."

Melvin stifled a laugh. "Glad to hear that, and I just happen to have extra meat in my packs. If you'd be good enough to tell me how you came to be here without a horse, I'd be honored to share some supper with you."

The boy sat up. "You've got a deal. I'll tell you just as soon as we're done eating."

Melvin stood, turned toward his supply packs and noted, "You sound hungry."

"Starving is a lot closer to the truth," the boy retorted.

Usually when people say they are starving, they're employing a figure of speech and really mean that they are hungry. However, in this case, the boy meant exactly what he said.

After retrieving a plate, a fork, and a second slab of beef from his packs, Melvin took a few moments to feed Mercy her oats. While he was thus occupied, the boy went to fetch a haversack and a saddle pad he'd stashed behind one of the cottonwoods. He and Melvin returned to the fire at the same moment, whereupon the boy produced a bowl, a spoon and two wrinkled potatoes from his tattered traveling bag. "They don't look like much," he offered, "but I've got a couple of spuds we can bake."

"Any spuds are better than none," said Melvin, setting down the items he was carrying. He then took a stick from the woodpile and reached for the bowie knife in the sheath on his left leg. He sharpened an end of the stick, impaled a beefsteak upon it and handed it to his guest. "Get the meat raring hot. That kills any varmints. Tastes better that way too."

"Mighty gentlemanly of you, Mister. Say, would it be too personal to ask your name?"

"Not at all. I'm Melvin Fitchett."

"Naw."

"What do you mean, naw? It's my name."

The boy scrutinized Melvin closely.

Melvin frowned. "What? You don't think I'd confuse my own name, do you?"

The boy shook his head in disbelief and turned to place the beef end of his stick over the fire. After a moment he replied, "No, I doubt you're confused. I'm just danged, that's all."

"And what are you danged about?" Melvin wondered. "My name doesn't usually upset people."

A smile crept into the corners of the boy's mouth and he

said, "I'm not upset. I'm danged because Melvin is my name too."

Now it was Melvin Fitchett's turn to look doubtful. "You're joshing me."

"No," the boy countered. "I've never met another Melvin before, but now that I have, I'm not about to josh him. Melvin Smyte is my name. It's been that since I remember."

Melvin Fitchett pried open the can of succotash with his big knife and placed the can on embers at the outer edge of the fire. "Durn."

The boy chuckled. "Now you know how I feel."

"Well . . . I reckon. It's nice to meet you, Melvin."

"Likewise, it's a pleasure."

"Hmmm. Think of the odds . . . two Melvins meeting out here in the middle of nowhere at night. I'd say that's some pretty wild luck."

Melvin Smyte withdrew his barely warm beefsteak from over the flame, bit off a chunk and swallowed without bothering to chew. "I don't know if it's wild luck or tame," he quipped slyly, "but it sure suits my stomach."

TWO

THE SUCCOTASH WAS divided evenly and they each grabbed a hot potato from beside the fire. Then, except for some appreciative lip-smacking and a couple of satisfied burps, the two Melvins consumed their meals in silence. Afterwards little Melvin put on his mostly dry shirt and took their dishes to the river to be washed. While the boy was gone, big Melvin unfurled his bedroll and placed his saddle on the sand for use as a backrest. He was cleaning his teeth with a twig when little Melvin returned and sat cross-legged by the fire.

It was a windless, star-sprinkled night, with the slim crescent of a new moon brightening the lower quadrant of the northwest sky. For several moments the pair sat without speaking and listened to the lulling song of the Red River. Way out on the prairie, a fox yapped twice, and soon the high-pitched bark was answered by a second fox, closer to camp. A moment later an owl, perched in one of the cottonwoods, hooted three times. The hooting seemed to unnerve little Melvin. He rotated toward the sound and peered apprehensively into the darkness. When the owl hooted a fourth time, he shuddered. Big Melvin had a hunch regarding the boy's fears and turned to look at Mercy. After she switched her tail lazily and bobbed her head, he informed his nervous guest, "You can relax. That was a fox and an owl. If it was Comanches, Mercy would've smelled their mounts."

Little Melvin wanted to be reassured, yet he was not quite convinced. "Maybe they're coming on foot."

"No. Comanches love to ride . . . especially when they attack. It's beneath their dignity to walk into battle."

When another vulpine yap resounded in the night, little Melvin noted, "It could be Apaches. Cochise might be after us."

"I doubt it. We're too far east for Apaches. Besides, I read in the newspaper that Cochise and President Grant were talking peace this spring."

"Maybe we should put the fire out anyway . . . just in case the talks didn't go well."

Big Melvin chuckled. "You might as well trust me. I know a fox when I hear one."

Little Melvin considered a moment, then acquiesced with a shrug. "I suspect you're right. I've seen several foxes in the past few days. There must be a den near here."

The boy's statement reminded big Melvin of the bargain

he'd struck before supper. "I believe you offered to tell me what you were doing here in the middle of nowhere without a horse."

"No." The boy shook his head. "I said I'd tell you how I got here, not what I was doing."

Melvin Fitchett smiled. "Pardon me."

The youngster shot a pointed look at big Melvin, then leaned forward, planted his elbows on his knees and rested his chin on the heels of his upturned hands. "You'll have to give me a few minutes to collect my thoughts. I've got a lot to remember since leaving Chicago last winter."

"Chicago? Didn't I read that it burned down last winter?"

Little Melvin scowled sideways at his host. Obviously, the boy did not approve of interruptions when he was collecting his thoughts. "I don't know what you read or what you didn't, Melvin. But yes, as a matter of fact, Chicago did burn down. Now, I'll leave it up to you. Do you want to talk or let me answer the question you asked?"

"Sorry. Go ahead."

Melvin Smyte remained with his elbows on his knees and his chin in his hands for a full five minutes without flinching or uttering a word. All during that time his face was taut with the inner concentration of someone looking back through time. Mercy and Melvin could not take their eyes off the boy. Both horse and man were impressed by his evident mental tenacity. Finally — after little Melvin had collected all of his thoughts and ordered them in his mind — he began telling the story of how he'd come to be sitting on the Great Staked Plains in north Texas. What he told was a condensed account of his journey, touching only upon the bolder facts while leaving many details unspoken. Nevertheless, it was a gripping tale, and below lies a materially faithful rendering of Melvin Smyte's story.

The boy's journey had started suddenly, without planning, late on a windy Sunday night in early October of the previous year. It began with a run over a bridge crowded with frantic citizens fleeing a burning city. Melvin's progress across the bridge was hampered by an older, less fleet companion named Slender Thomas. The pair spent that night wandering along the banks of the Des Plaines River, which led them to the Illinois River, and then shortly after dawn the next morning, they stowed away on a lumber barge heading for points south. Three days later Melvin and Slender Thomas disembarked in St. Louis, Missouri, where they survived a long, rough winter hawking homemade cough medicine to ailing pedestrians on the streets. The following spring the pair had booked passage on a Mississippi River steamboat bound for Natchez. In Natchez they transferred to a smaller paddleboat that continued down the

Mississippi until it reached the mouth of the Red River, where it turned west and proceeded to the recently incorporated town of Shreveport, Louisiana, the end of the line for passenger boats. The twosome disembarked in Shreveport intending to locate Slender Thomas's baby sister, Cora. Slender Thomas had not seen or heard from Cora in twenty-two years, but he'd dreamed she was living in Shreveport and had his heart set on a reunion. A week went by without finding so much as a trace of Cora . . . and then Slender Thomas's strength began to abandon him. From there the situation had gone from dour to dire . . . until ultimately it reached such a sorrowful pitch that little Melvin could not presently bear to recall the facts and lapsed into a glum silence.

Big Melvin was of course curious about what had happened in Shreveport, yet he dared not agitate the boy while he was busy thinking and refrained from asking any questions.

After an extended pause, little Melvin heaved a forlorn sigh and leaped abruptly to the end of his tale. "So . . . I bought a skewbald gelding from a horse trader with one eye, got my gear together and rode out of town. His name is Ben."

Big Melvin, sensing that it was now safe to speak, wondered, "Who? The one-eyed horse trader?"

"No. Ben is my horse. I never learned the trader's name."

"I see. What kind of horse?"

"A pony, actually. The one-eyed man said he was an Oglala Sioux Buffalo runner. That's special."

Big Melvin nodded. "Buffalo runners are hard to find."

"Anyway," little Melvin continued, "I've been following the Red River just like Slender Thomas told me to do. I'm looking for the Chisholm Trail. Probably would have found it by now if some thieving Comanches hadn't run off with Ben."

Melvin Fitchett doubted that Comanches were involved with the boy's missing pony, but he didn't express the sentiment. He did, however, inform the youngster, "You passed the trail. It's at least a dozen miles east of here."

"Naw."

"Yeah. There's a cattle station on the river where the trail leaves Texas. It's a pretty sizeable operation. I don't know how you missed it."

A frustrated moan arose from little Melvin and he slapped at the ground with both hands. "Of all the rotten luck. Wouldn't you know it! I take one day to ride out on the prairie and look around, and that's when I miss my mark."

"Luck can be funny sometimes."

"Ha, ha, ha. I'm laughing now."

Big Melvin ignored the boy's sarcasm. This was the frontier west and it did not pay to take offense at contradictory humor. He cleared his throat and asked, "When did you lose Ben?"

"Two nights ago. I was sleeping right under him, and the next morning when I woke up, he was gone. Those Comanches are sneaky devils, let me tell you. I didn't hear a thing."

Big Melvin decided to steer clear of the Comanche question and satisfy his curiosity about another matter. "So, Melvin . . . how old are you? Thirteen? Fourteen?"

Melvin Smyte furrowed his brow and glowered at big Melvin as if the man had slapped his face. "You trying to get me riled?"

"No. Just asking an innocent question."

The boy rolled his eyes, got to his knees, shuffled over to within a foot of big Melvin and pointed at his upper lip. "See that?"

Big Melvin squinted. Maybe he saw some grime. "I, ah . . . I'm not sure what you mean."

Little Melvin huffed, shook his head and announced, "The light from this fire is so poor, you probably can't see it. But I've got a brown mustache."

Big Melvin did his best to limit the smile that appeared on his face. "Oh, yeah, sure. I see that. It's a mustache."

Little Melvin withdrew to his previous spot beside the fire and recrossed his legs. "I'm sixteen."

"Sixteen, huh?"

"I know I'm on the small side, but don't let that throw you. Plenty of people are small."

Melvin Fitchett could remember what it meant to be young and was quick to agree. "Oh yeah. I knew a fellow in Virginia that wasn't much bigger than a midget, and he was tough as nails."

"I'm way bigger than a midget."

"Oh, yeah."

"Now let me guess. You're thirty."

"Twenty-seven."

Little Melvin nodded. "I knew that. I just added a few years to be polite."

"Thanks." Big Melvin lost control of his smile.

Little Melvin turned and peered ponderously into the fire. After a moment he volunteered, "Seeing as we have the same name and all, Melvin, I reckon I can tell you what I'm doing here. I've been prospecting for gold."

"Gold? On the Red River? Don't believe I've heard of any gold strikes in Texas."

"And that's why I'm looking here," little Melvin offered with alacrity, then explained, "Everybody's already rushed to Colorado and Nevada and California. I figured I'd start somewhere new. That way, if there's gold to be found, I'll be the first to arrive."

Big Melvin could only admire the boy's logic. "There's an original plan."

"Don't tell anyone."

"I won't."

Little Melvin yawned, uncrossed his legs and reached for his soot-stained blanket. "I'll take your word on that, Melvin. Now, unless you've got more questions, I'm tired. I think I'll turn in for the night."

"Make yourself comfy," big Melvin replied, adding, "It's not a question, but I do have a comment I'd like to make."

The boy spread his blanket on the sand by the fire, grabbed his saddle pad for use as a pillow, stretched out on his side and said, "Go ahead, comment."

"Well . . . I've noticed that you speak properly. No ain'ts, or weren'ts, or done-did-thats out of your mouth."

"That was Miss Prescott's doing. She ran the orphanage where I grew up. Miss Prescott was a stickler about grammar. She always said good usage would get me places."

Big Melvin was favorably impressed. "Hats off to Miss Prescott."

"I can read too," little Melvin whispered sleepily. "Now good night."

"Good night," echoed Melvin Fitchett. He lay his head

upon his saddle, gazed up at the stars and wondered: Where is Evelyn? And when he finished contemplating that unanswerable question, he wondered if he would sleep peacefully or dream the ghostly dream that had been haunting him on and off since the Battle of Wilderness in 1864. The dream was always the same: a nightmare filled with horrific images that never varied. Sometimes it stayed away a month or more, and once it left him be for a whole summer, yet it was always there . . . looming in the dark like an irresistible monster from which he could not hide. In that sense, for Melvin, sleep was a gamble he took every night.

THREE

THE MORNING SUN inched over the horizon, streaked across the plains, peeked between two cottonwoods and tickled the tips of Melvin Fitchett's eyelashes. They were long lashes, darker than the nutmeg-brown hair on his head, and they parted to reveal pastel-blue eyes. He sat up and looked around. There was no sign of his new friend. All he saw was Mercy, watching him. If a horse can be said to smile, that is what she did. He greeted her with a nod and reached for his lucky hat, a ginger-colored, felt sombrero. He put on the hat, pulled on his socks and boots, stood and gave Mercy an affectionate slap on the rump. "Go graze for thirty or forty minutes, then come back here."

Mercy indicated with a snort that she understood before lumbering up the tree-lined bank and trotting onto the plain. After she went, Melvin sorted through his supply packs, taking out a tin pot, an iron skillet, a packet of bacon and a small sack of coffee. He gathered some twigs and chips of bark, lay them on the ashes of the past night's fire and coached a flame into existence. After adding a few sticks to the flame he went to fill the tin pot with water.

Everywhere Melvin looked along the riverbank the sand

had been scratched, panned, pitted and tossed aside in disorderly piles. Melvin moaned. He knew any trout larger than a minnow had fled to calmer waters the moment the boy began prospecting. Oh, well, Melvin Fitchett mused. At least I won't have to chase grasshoppers for bait. He kneeled, filled his tin pot and was splashing water on his face when a voice called to him from downstream, "There you are. I thought you were going to sleep all day."

Melvin Fitchett picked up the pot of water and stood. "I see you found your derby."

"Yep. It was floating upside down in an eddy. I'm wearing it wet so it doesn't shrink."

"Good idea. You in a mood for breakfast?"

Little Melvin placed both hands on his stomach and feigned indecisiveness. He hesitated briefly, then pretended to receive a signal from his stomach and answered, "Well, yes, it seems I am in the mood for breakfast."

Big Melvin smirked and ambled back to the fire.

Moments later the two Melvins had eaten and the smaller one was pouring coffee into a tin cup he'd taken from his haversack when he froze and looked around in alarm. Suddenly he blurted, "Melvin. Mercy is gone! The Comanches got your horse."

Big Melvin replied calmly, "No, they didn't. I sent Mercy out to graze for a spell. She'll be back in fifteen minutes."

Little Melvin finished filling his cup, set the tin pot on the ground and grinned. "Fifteen minutes, unh? Don't tell me your horse carries a watch."

"Okay. I won't."

"Good, because I wouldn't believe it if I saw it."

"Mercy is smart and she always does what I tell her. Just wait. She'll be back on time."

The boy rolled his light brown eyes. "I'll be danged. I just ate breakfast with a madman."

Melvin Fitchett frowned. He was not amused.

Melvin Smyte chuckled.

The older Melvin sipped coffee and continued frowning. After a moment he set down his cup, reached into one of his supply packs, withdrew a wad of soft paper and got to his feet. "Excuse me. I've got business around the bend."

When big Melvin returned, little Melvin greeted him with a smug look and observed, "Your horse should have been back by now. It's been over fifteen minutes."

"More like ten, I'd say."

"Oh, right," the boy remarked testily. "I know your type. You hate to admit when you're wrong."

Big Melvin looked blandly at the boy, got back on his feet and gestured north beyond the cottonwoods. "Let's have a look. I suspect she's on her way back by now."

The twosome climbed out of the river bottom and

walked onto the plains, where their view was unobstructed for as many miles as the eye could see. Almost immediately they saw a speck in the distance. Next to it was a smaller speck. "Hold on a second," big Melvin said, whirling about and hurrying back to camp. A moment later when he returned to little Melvin's side he was carrying a twelve-inch, black metal telescope. He lifted the instrument to an eye, fiddled with the lens and soon thereafter announced, "It's Mercy . . . and it appears she's found a friend. They're coming this way."

"A friend?"

"Yeah . . . looks like a pony, black with white splotches. Did you tell me Ben was a skewbald?"

"Give me that spyglass."

Big Melvin did not respond.

"I mean, lend it to me. Please."

Big Melvin handed over the telescope and grinned. "Don't that beat all. First the Comanches stole your pony. Then they turned around and set him free."

Little Melvin studied the magnified image of his missing pony for several seconds, handed the telescope back to big Melvin and grumbled, "Maybe Ben escaped."

"I hadn't thought of that." Big Melvin chuckled. "Sure. It could have happened."

Little Melvin knew when he was being mocked. He

flashed an offended look at big Melvin, clamped his jaw shut and did not speak until after Ben and Mercy had crossed the plains and came to a halt in front of their waiting owners. Then the youngster stepped forward to scratch his pony's forehead and said, "I don't know where you've been, Ben, but you've got to be more careful about the friends you pick up with. That horse you're with belongs to a cruel man."

Big Melvin snorted. "What's cruel about me? All I've done so far is feed you supper and breakfast."

Little Melvin willfully ignored the question and continued to stroke Ben's forehead.

Melvin Fitchett was a man of manners who tolerated only so much rudeness from others. He did not know why the boy insisted on being so disagreeable, but he did, and big Melvin was miffed. He clicked his tongue for Mercy to come, spun on his heels and started toward the river bottom. He neither cared nor looked over his shoulder to see if the stubborn boy followed or not.

The recently retired cowpoke washed his dishes, tin pot and skillet in the river, filled his canteen and parfleche water bag, threw sand on the firepit, tied up a bundle of sticks for future use and began packing his gear for departure. He was adjusting the girth strap on Mercy's saddle when Ben and Melvin Smyte descended the north bank, strolled onto the peninsula and walked silently past him to the river. As the pony drank thirstily, the boy stood with hands in his pockets and gazed south toward Texas. From all that could be read from his manner, little Melvin wasn't the least bit concerned whether big Melvin was leaving or staying put.

Big Melvin could play the aloof game as well: He secured his packs and bundle of wood on Mercy's rump, rested his encased rifle between the two packs and swung into the saddle. He sat for a moment, gazing at Melvin Smyte's back. Slowly, the boy turned and acknowledged Melvin Fitchett with a sanguine look. "So, I see you're leaving."

"Yeah . . . it's that time."

"Unhuh. It always comes eventually."

"It does." Big Melvin touched the brim of his hat. "Good luck prospecting."

Not only did the time to go always come eventually, but so did the time to make amends, and Melvin Smyte was acutely aware that the latter moment had arrived. His demeanor changed from cool to warm and the light in his brown eyes softened. "Melvin . . . I hate to see you rush off. I know I'm ornery sometimes. Slender Thomas said I could aggravate a rock. I don't mean to be that way. I just am."

Melvin Fitchett held his reins slack. He was curious to hear what the boy might say next.

The youngster dropped his eyes, kicked obsequiously at the sand and offered, "It's not easy being me, so I'm not going to beg, but I doubt I'll meet another Melvin anytime soon . . . and if I do, I'm sure he won't need a partner as much as you."

"I need a partner!?"

Little Melvin looked up and nodded. "After hearing you talk in your sleep last night, I believe you do."

Big Melvin's spine stiffened, his shoulders tensed and his face twitched with anger. "That's putting your nose where it doesn't belong."

"Now don't get riled," little Melvin advised in a diplomatic tone. "I didn't sneak listen. It just happened. I was asleep when you woke me up talking. I've got ears. I couldn't help but hear what you said."

Big Melvin swallowed what may have been a curse word.

Little Melvin shifted his feet and hooked his hands behind his back. "Anyways . . . somebody is obviously after you. A good partner could watch your back."

Big Melvin grimaced and rolled his blue eyes upward. "No one is after me."

"No? Then who is Ezekiel?"

For several long seconds Melvin Fitchett gazed at a solitary white cloud floating high in the western sky. Tension suddenly drained from his body. He turned to the boy and spoke in a voice that cracked with emotion. "Ezekiel Beck was my friend. I must've had another nightmare about the war. I suppose I talk sometimes when I have that dream."

After a respectful pause, little Melvin wondered, "Were you a Yankee or a Rebel?"

"I was a Confederate soldier, in the Army of Northern Virginia."

"Oh." Little Melvin dropped his hands from behind his back and let them dangle at his side. "Sorry about you guys losing. I'm sure it wasn't your fault."

There are no words to describe the pained look that flashed across Melvin Fitchett's long face. Suffice it to say that he had suffered numerous mental and physical bruises in the war.

Little Melvin coughed to clear the air and stepped forward. "If there was any gold here, I would've found it by now. But I haven't, so there's no use in me staying. What do you say we ride together?"

"Hmmm."

"Hmmm what?"

"You don't even know where I'm going."

"Where doesn't matter."

"It does to most people. I'm going pretty far."

"All right then. We'll ride to the nearest town. You can ditch me whenever you want."

Big Melvin paused, pursed his lips and considered.

"I've got fourteen dollars and change. I'll pay for food."

Just my luck to find an orphan, thought Melvin Fitchett, and after sighing, he said, "There's supposed to be a new town on the Kansas border, called Caldwell. I hear it's a rough little place, but I'll probably stop there for a night."

Little Melvin assumed the air of a humble supplicant.

"There's nothing but open Indian country between here and Kansas."

An irrepressible smile crept into the corners of the boy's mouth. He could feel wind blowing in his direction. "I wouldn't be here if I was daunted by Indians."

Big Melvin rubbed his stubbled chin. "How about your pony? Does Ben have good shoes?"

"I took him to a blacksmith before I left Shreveport."

An amused sort of grin appeared on big Melvin's face and he informed the boy, "You can ride with me on one condition."

"What?"

"One Melvin is enough for any crowd, so I'm giving you a nickname. It'll save on confusion if and when we encounter other people."

"And what is it?"

"Whittle."

"Whittle! What kind of name is that?"

Big Melvin chuckled. "Just something I made up. It suits you, though. You'll get used to it."

Little Melvin (or rather, Whittle) gritted his teeth and glared defiantly at the tall, slim man on the horse.

"You coming or not?"

For an instant it looked as if the boy might explode, or cry, or maybe attack his new partner, but then he exhaled loudly and replied, "I'm coming. Just sit tight while I collect my gear and put my saddle pad on Ben."

FOUR

THE SUN WAS more than two hours into its daily journey when Melvin Fitchett and Melvin "Whittle" Smyte exited the river bottom and rode onto the plain beyond the cottonwoods. It was no ordinary plain. They were on the North American Great Plains, a stretch of arid topography that begins in south Texas and extends nearly fifteen hundred miles north through the Dakotas and into Canada. Except for a few minor hills scattered here and there, flat is the dominant theme of the Great Plains. For the most part they are carpeted in tall, tough gama grass that occasionally gives way to patches of scrub chaparral, thorny bushes and small leaf briars. The only trees to be found on the Great Plains are in those places where mountain-shed rivers course through the land en route to the Gulf of Mexico.

Immense herds of migrating buffalo once wandered hither and thither on the plains, but by the spring of 1872 as the two Melvins set out together, the great bison herds no longer existed south of the Platte River in Nebraska. This pitiful development was due to the rapidly expanding railroads which had begun hauling white hunters to the frontier in 1869. Those bloodthirsty killers with their long rifles — they managed to decimate the migrating herds in less than three years. Where once millions of beasts had roamed, all that remained in 1872 were a few isolated groups of thirty to forty buffalo at most.

Melvin, concerned more about distance than time, held Mercy to a slow trot over the grass-covered flatness. Ben proved to be a hardy pony and had no apparent trouble keeping up with the tall Kentucky mare. Periodically, the horses snorted or whinnied to each other. Were they discussing the partnership their masters had formed, or just making equine noises? Or, as Melvin wondered, were they trying to tell their riders something? With each whinny or snort, he cast a precautionary glance to the east, the west and the south behind them. Otherwise he gazed silently northward and followed a line of private thoughts in that direction.

They rode all morning without stopping, pushed through the noon hour and proceeded into the heat of the day. Credit to Ben and to Whittle: The pony never tarried far from Mercy's lead and the boy voiced no complaints about his dust-filled nostrils, his dry mouth, his irritated eyes or his sore bottom. He was determined to pass whatever endurance test Melvin Fitchett saw fit to administer.

Late that afternoon, with the sun long past its zenith in the sky, Melvin swerved from his northern tack and headed toward a dry gulch that had suddenly revealed itself on the plain. The gulch ran south to north, and the base of its western slope was cast in shadows. He stopped in the shade, dismounted and was taking the bridle from Mercy's mouth when Whittle and Ben came to a halt a few feet away. Whittle eyed Melvin curiously. "You're stopping already? Don't tell me you're tired. We've only been riding since morning."

"Mercy is thirsty. So am I."

Whittle responded with a haughty expression that said he knew an excuse when he heard one.

"You can keep going if you want," Melvin informed the boy.

Whittle dismounted and dropped his knapsack to the ground. "A short break won't hurt me. I suspect Ben is thirsty too."

Melvin grabbed his water bag, removed his sombrero, set the hat on the ground in front of Mercy and half filled the impromptu container. Afterwards he motioned to Whittle, indicating that he would pour water for Ben if the boy set his hat down. Whittle approved of the idea, but when he attempted to remove his black derby — which had soaked all night in the river, then baked all day in the sun — he discovered that it was stuck to his head. It wasn't permanently stuck, yet it fit so snugly Whittle had to fight for thirty seconds before the hat popped free.

Melvin Fitchett threw back his head and laughed, but his mirth was short-lived, as the boy suddenly swooned, stumbled sideways and fell to the ground in a faint. Melvin dropped to a knee and anxiously inspected the youngster, whose eyes had rolled back in his head. Two dousings of water, three lightly applied slaps on the face and four minutes later Whittle Smyte's brown eyes returned to their normal position and slowly regained their focus. "Are you all right?" asked Melvin.

"Ahhh," the boy moaned weakly.

Melvin held up a hand. "How many fingers?"

"Four," Whittle whispered. "Five if I count your thumb."

Melvin handed his canteen to the boy. "Here. Do you need help sitting up?"

"Naw, I can make it." Whittle sat up slowly and drank. "Do me a favor, would you?"

"Sure."

"Reach into the back pocket on my haversack and fetch me the brown bottle."

Melvin found the requested bottle and before handing it to the boy he took a look at the label, which read:

SLENDER TOM'S MIRACLE COUGH TONIC

25 CENTS

ONE SMALL DOSE DISPATCHES ALL AILMENTS OF THE CHEST

SECRET INGREDIENTS — GUARANTEED RESULTS

Whittle removed the cork from the bottle, took a swig of

its contents, then soon exclaimed, "WINGDIGGITY!" His body convulsed from head to toe, his eyes bulged in their sockets, his teeth chattered and his face turned beet red. Then he burped and sighed with relief. He was revived.

Melvin reached to take the bottle from Whittle's hand and sniffed its contents. The odor sent his head rearing back. "Lord, what's in this stuff?"

The boy got to his feet and brushed the dust from his clothes. "I can't tell you. I was sworn to secrecy."

Melvin shook his head in amazement. "Well, whatever is in there, it appears to have worked a miracle on you."

"Yep, it's powerful medicine," Whittle concurred, bending to pick up his derby. He gave the hat a reproachful look, then shrugged and said to Melvin, "What the heck. I don't suppose the secret matters to Slender Thomas anymore. It's made with ginger root, cayenne pepper, garlic, lemon juice, a plug of tobacco and crushed bumblebee bottoms."

Melvin looked doubtful. "Bumblebee bottoms?"

Whittle affirmed the fact with a nod. "Dried and crushed. I was in charge of collecting the bees."

Melvin was verily impressed. "In all my travels, I never heard of such."

"You never heard of it because you never met Slender Thomas. The man was a genius. He was sitting on a curb one day and the recipe just leapt into his head."

"Wow. So what happened in Shreveport? You never told me."

Whittle looked down and studied the inside of his derby for a moment before answering, "Well . . . basically, Slender Thomas lay down one night and gave up the ghost."

"So sorry to hear that." Melvin paused, and when Whittle did not speak, he wondered, "What'd the man die from?"

Whittle raised his head to look at Melvin, sighed sadly, peered back down at his hat and said, "It's hard to know exactly what got Slender Thomas. He was pretty old and had a lot of things that ached inside. If I had to guess, though, I'd say he died of disappointments. They'd been piling up on him pretty rapidly near the end."

There were many ways to die, thought Melvin: A bullet could smack you in the forehead. You could fall from a horse and break your neck. You could drown in a river. And now, he had learned, you could die of disappointments. He picked up his water bag and told Whittle, "Put your hat down. Ben is looking mighty thirsty."

"I've got a better idea." The boy set his derby lightly on his head, strode over to his haversack, put the cough tonic in its keeping place, opened the top flap and withdrew his wooden bowl. "Here. Use this. I'd rather not get my lid wet again."

Melvin chortled and filled the bowl. After Ben quickly

lapped up its contents, he filled it again. Then he turned to pour another half-hat full for Mercy, set the water bag on the ground, looked at the sky and observed, "It'll be getting dark in about an hour."

"Yeah," Whittle rejoined. "The day slipped right by."

"We came a fair bit. Unless you have any objections, let's settle here for the night. The gulch will hide our fire."

"Hide . . . you mean from Indians?"

"From whatever." Melvin refused to get specific. "A man can see pretty far across these plains. No use sending out a beacon saying we're here. Besides, I like keeping Mercy fresh when I'm in strange territory."

Whittle's eyes widened with comprehension and he rotated his head to survey the surroundings. "Then let's settle. I, ah . . . I see you're carrying a rifle case. Something in it, I suppose."

"A Sharps Fifty Caliber. It's a good long gun."

Whittle nodded. "So, what you got for close range?"

"Nothing."

"Nothing?" The boy sounded an incredulous note. "You must have a pistol tucked away somewhere."

As was his habit when perturbed, Melvin Fitchett stiffened. "Are your ears clean? I said nothing. Pistols are for desperate men with itchy fingers. I'm no gunfighter, Whittle, if that's what you're getting at."

The boy was surprised by Melvin's heated response and he quickly replied, "I wasn't getting at anything. I was only wondering about your resources in case trouble jumped us."

In the time it takes to spell the word flash, Melvin slid his bowie knife from its sheath, flipped it in the air and caught it cleanly by the handle. "I'm pretty handy with this if trouble starts jumping."

"Right. Good. I don't doubt you."

Melvin returned his knife to its sheath and began removing his supplies and saddle from Mercy's back. When he was done he sat on a rock with his back against the shaded wall of the gulch, sighed and offered reflectively, "Take it from me, Whittle, close fighting is ugly business. I ought to know. I didn't join up until halfway through the war, when I was eighteen, but the first action I saw was at Gettysburg, which opened my eyes, let me tell you . . . yet it wasn't nearly as ugly as Wilderness. In three days at Wilderness I saw more dead men than you could make up names for, and I saw them close. I won't try to describe what it felt like, because I can't, but Wilderness changed something inside of me that won't ever change back. Anyway, my point is, Whittle, it's a policy of mine not to carry pistols. The way folks are, out here in the West, pistols invite trouble."

The boy nodded. He understood. He also sensed that if push came to shove, Melvin Fitchett could take care of himself, one way or the other. "So, Wilderness was the ugly one, unh?"

"It was hell."

"That where you got the scar on your forehead?"

Melvin reached to touch the horizontal scar above his left eyebrow. "Yep. And if it wasn't for dumb luck and a fraction of an inch, I wouldn't be here today. Now that's all I want to say about the matter. It's time I build a fire and cook supper. Same menu as last night. That suit you?"

"It does."

A short while later, after the travelers had eaten and were watching the fire dwindle, Whittle informed Melvin, "I've been thinking two things all day. They both need considering."

"Oh? What are they?"

"I'll start with a question. Why aren't we following the Chisholm Trail? If I've got my bearings straight, we're going in the same direction."

"We are," Melvin confirmed, but that was all he said.

"So why? Are you avoiding the law or something?" asked Whittle, adding quickly, "I know that's two questions, but I count them as one."

Melvin smiled. He had nothing to hide. "I was a cowhand for nearly four years. Worked on a ranch near Fort

Concho, Texas. In fact, I only quit the job a few days before we met. Anyhow, I've ridden the Chisholm Trail from Fort Concho to Abilene, Kansas, and back on two different occasions and it gets pretty thick with cattle at this time of year. I don't know if you've ever gotten behind a big herd before, but if you have and the wind started blowing in the wrong direction, then you know the dust can choke you to death from five miles away. And that's just one reason to avoid the trail. It also attracts a fair share of bandits. They're drawn to the drovers carrying money and supplies . . . not to mention the lure of fresh beef."

"I see," observed the boy. "Although you still didn't tell whether you were avoiding the law or not."

Melvin gave Whittle a hurt look. He didn't like being pegged as a criminal. "I'm clean with the law. Only crime I committed was waiting so long to quit my job. Now, what was the other thing on your mind?"

Whittle hooked his hands behind his head and leaned back against the wall of the gulch. "I was thinking our terms aren't right."

"What terms?"

"Our name terms. It's not fair, you calling me Whittle while you get to keep Melvin, which is my name too. At least it was, once upon a time."

Melvin chuckled.

"Laugh all you want," Whittle informed his lanky companion. "From now on I'm calling you Stick."

"Stick?"

"It suits you," Whittle asserted testily. "Remember? That's what you said when you nicknamed me."

"Stick. Hmmm. That's got a ring to it. I like it."

Whittle huffed. "You just like it because I'm better at giving nicknames than you are."

Melvin Fitchett laughed and began to take off his boots. "Don't blame me, Whittle. Everyone has different talents."

"Right, Stick, and you're good at being cruel."

"Huh."

"Huh all you want. It's true."

FIVE

STICK AND WHITTLE were up at the first hint of dawn, and having burned their supply of wood the night before, they skipped breakfast and rode from the gulch before the bottom arc of the sun lifted over the horizon. The prairie was flat and still for as far as the eye could see, and except for the bottom of the sky lying upon the ground, it was an empty, silent, dominant vastness that hinted at the duo's relative insignificance in the world. Humbled by the plain, they did not speak. Nor did the horses attempt to communicate. Mile after mile, the only sounds were the muffled clopping of hooves on a grass-padded surface and the occasional creaking of Stick's leather saddle. All the while the sun climbed steadily higher and grew hotter and hotter.

They had been riding for three hours and Whittle had just concluded that one could ride forever on the plains and never see another living creature when a panicked roadrunner suddenly ran out of nowhere and zigzagged wildly ahead of the travelers. The crazed bird darted this way and that for nearly a mile before abruptly and mysteriously disappearing into a hole, or into thin air, or to somewhere that Whittle could not guess.

As three hours became four and four became five, the essence of time succumbed to the concept of distance and the notion of getting anywhere seemed truly preposterous. Everything was far and everything under the rock-baking sun glimmered heat.

It was toward the end of their fifth hour traveling when Whittle rode forth on Ben and drew even with Stick. He licked his dry lips, swallowed grit and asked, "What are we doing for water? I haven't got more than a slosh left in my canteen."

"Save it."

Whittle spit cotton. "For how long, you reckon?"

"We should hit the Washita tomorrow. I'm hoping we find water before then."

"What are our chances?"

"That depends whether we get lucky or not."

As Whittle's tone made clear, he was far from satisfied with his partner's answer. "In that case, mind telling me if you feel lucky today?"

Stick cocked an eye at Whittle. "It depends again. Are you asking a philosophical question, or a practical one?"

"Practical," Whittle snapped. "Do you think we'll find water or not?"

Stick replied with amusement. "Well, let's see . . . I slept rather soundly last night. That's usually a good sign. And as a rule, I tend toward optimism. So — speaking strictly from my gut, you understand — I'd say our chances of lucking upon water are fair to middling."

Whittle moaned and let Ben fall back in line behind Mercy. After a minute or so, he called ahead, "Remind me never to ask you a simple question again."

Stick chuckled. "If you're thirsty, Whittle, you ought not to talk so much. Words use up moisture when you say them."

"If that's true, you must be dryer than dust."

The word luck, as a noun, is defined in most dictionaries as "a force that brings good fortune or adversity." As a verb-in-transit it becomes "to prosper or succeed, especially through chance." Melvin Fitchett's appreciation of the word went deeper than dictionaries. He honored luck and revered its influence in the world. Something had saved him during the long night of hell at Wilderness where men had died around him at the rate of three thousand per hour, and the only way he could name that something was to call it divine intervention or luck. Being neither a pious nor religious man in practice, he was more at ease crediting luck. For him it was a safer word, yet no less mysterious for being so.

At any rate, whatever the word: Here he was, alive, baking in the midday sun on the Great Plains of the western frontier. He may not have fully comprehended why he survived while so many others did not, but he knew what he was living for, and her name was Evelyn Laroue. Finding her was his driving purpose. Ah, Evelyn, with her walnut-brown hair and her apple-green eyes. No one could make the birds sing like Evelyn.

Poor Evelyn. Her father had died early in the war, in a senseless skirmish at Hanging Rock, Virginia, and within the week her mother's already fragile mind had cracked and disassembled. A year or so later Melvin had donned the gray and marched to Lee's aid. Some eighteen hellish months after that Evelyn had been erroneously informed that her brave young sweetheart met his demise at Wilderness. Evelyn had fled her home in tears, refusing to reside any longer in the devastated dominion that held so many wretched memories for her.

After the war, following clues from the one letter she had written to her mother in the sanitorium, Melvin had tracked Evelyn to a boardinghouse in Baltimore, where her trail had gone cold. The matron of the place thought she recollected Evelyn accepting a governess position with a family that was heading out west, yet she couldn't recall the family name. "It may have been French," the woman allowed, although she wasn't entirely certain if she was recollecting Evelyn or someone else.

Melvin had not seen Evelyn since May of 1864. The face

he remembered belonged to a seventeen-year-old girl, who he knew must be a woman by now. However, he chose not to imagine her that way. Women got married and, well, Melvin preferred to remember Evelyn as he'd left her standing in the lane outside her home so many long years ago.

The past was gone. Melvin knew that. He just wanted to find Evelyn and show her he was alive.

Melvin "Stick" Fitchett noticed a dot soaring high in the sky and was suddenly drawn from his reveries. The dot was several thousand yards west of where he and Whittle were riding, and as he studied its circular movements, he perceived that the dot was a hawk. Without hesitating he reined Mercy to his left and started across the prairie toward a band of low-lying hills.

Whittle had no idea why they'd abruptly altered course, yet it was apparent that Stick knew why and where he was going, and Whittle followed without question.

Stick rode to the foot of the hills, halted, dismounted and took his telescope from a bag. He turned to Whittle, touched a finger to his lips and started on foot into the hills. Whittle dropped to the ground, told Ben to stay with Mercy and hurried after Stick. They moved swiftly up the eastern slope of the hills, crouched as they approached the crest and dropped onto all fours just shy of the summit. Stick tapped Whittle on the arm, signalled for the boy to stay put and remain silent, removed his hat, inched forward on his stomach and peeked over the hilltop. Down below, some sixty yards to the west, stood a thicket of briars, bushes and tall reed grasses. To Stick's experienced eye, the dense growth indicated the presence of a spring. He remained low to the ground, cautiously lifted his telescope and surveyed the scene.

Although Whittle tried waiting patiently for Stick to report his findings, within less than a minute he lost control of his curiosity and whispered, "What is it? Comanches?"

Stick had half a mind to spin around and box the boy on his ears, but he did not move, for just then the bird of prey rolled, dove down from the heavens and shot into the thicket. There was a squeal, a screech, a rustling in the thicket . . . then the hawk lifted skyward with a struggling rabbit in its talons. Stick sighed in awe, and with relief. He knew the hawk would not have descended if any humans were lying in ambush. He turned and told Whittle, "We're in luck. We found a spring. It looks all clear to me."

"Good going," Whittle said unenthusiastically.

"You don't sound pleased."

"I am." Whittle shrugged. "It's just that I was a little bit hoping we'd surprise some Indians."

Stick was somewhat puzzled and he wondered, "Why would you hope that?"

Whittle hesitated briefly before confessing, "Because

I've never seen a wild Indian and I want to see one before the disease does them all in."

Stick was now perplexed. "Disease? What do you mean? The smallpox epidemic was thirty years ago."

"I'm talking about man-infested-density. Slender Thomas told me about it. I think it's a problem in their blood."

Stick pondered a moment. Suddenly he threw back his head and laughed. It was a moment before he could catch his breath and speak. "You must have heard wrong. I believe what Slender Thomas actually said was *Manifest Destiny*."

"That might be it," Whittle agreed. "It sounds right."

Stick enjoyed another fit of laughter. Eventually he managed to explain, "Manifest Destiny isn't a disease. It's an idea, or rather a doctrine intended to express our rights as Americans to go where we want and make progress. It says 'Go west and claim the frontiers' and argues that our right to do so was allotted by Providence."

"Never heard of it."

"You wouldn't unless you read the newspapers regularly . . . or listened to politicians giving speeches in Washington. Manifest Destiny tells us to forget the war we just fought and turn our attention to settling new places."

Whittle hemmed. "Wonder why Slender Thomas told me it was killing Indians? He was pretty smart."

"Well . . ." Stick thought for a second. "In a roundabout

way, Slender Thomas was right. Manifest Destiny does harm the Indians when politicians use it as a reason for breaking treaties and taking away the Indian homelands."

There was an element of newfound respect in Whittle's eyes as he looked at Stick. He was weighing the man in a whole new light. "Are you a scholar or something?"

"No." Stick smiled modestly.

"Then how do you know all this stuff?"

"I read a lot, and I did attend William and Mary College for two years before I entered the war. I suppose I learned a few things there, but I'm no scholar. Far from it."

Whittle was visibly impressed. "Still, you've been educated, Stick. I admire educated people."

"Thank you."

"I aim to learn what comes my way. That's my approach."

Stick nodded. "There's a lot to be said for that."

"As for that Manifest Whatever-you-call-it, if it's harming Indians, it isn't much of an idea, is it?"

"I suppose not." Stick got to his feet and extended a hand down to Whittle. "Come on, partner. Let's go wet our whistles."

"Let's," agreed the orphaned youngster. He liked being called partner.

SIX

STICK AND WHITTLE reached the Washita River shortly before noon the next day. It wasn't much of a river. Indeed, as Whittle remarked upon crossing, "This little trickle should be proud to call itself a creek."

They dismounted in a cluster of sandbar willows and let their horses forage while they scrounged for firewood. Over forty hours had passed since they'd eaten a cooked meal and they had designs on the remaining two beefsteaks in Stick's pack. Ample wood was soon found and a fire lit. However, the hungry duo might have spared themselves the effort, for they consumed the meat in lupine fashion before it was thoroughly hot.

Whittle burped when he was done. "Delicious."

"It was," Stick agreed. "I reckon we'll be relying on nature between here and Caldwell."

Whittle huffed. "Not counting the roadrunner and the hawk by the spring, I haven't seen much nature."

"Look around," said Stick. "Everything you see is nature."

"I meant *eating* nature," Whittle shot back. "And don't tell me grass is food. I'm no buffalo."

A broad grin appeared on Stick's face.

Whittle leaned back and cocked his derby over his brow. "So, you've decided on Caldwell. Is that where you plan to ditch me?"

The grin disappeared from Stick's face. "I haven't made such plans."

"Are you saying you're not going to ditch me?"

Stick rolled his eyes. "I will if you won't listen. I just told you, I haven't made any plans."

"Okay. Don't get riled."

Stick released an exasperated sigh, paused, then offered, "For what it's worth, Whittle, here lately it's seemed to me that friends are getting hard to find. Now that could be a consequence of my doing, or else I haven't been meeting many likeable people. Anyhow . . . we only hitched up a couple of days ago, yet it's been my opinion that we were getting along well."

Whittle sat up slowly and adjusted his hat. "Let me get this straight. Are you saying we're friends?"

"Sure. Why not?"

Suddenly, Whittle's face lit with an emotion that emphasized his youthful innocence. He was more than happy. He was honored. "I'm big on friends myself. I've never had what anyone could call a proper family."

Stick was touched. He caught a frog in his throat and

swallowed. "Well then, let's keep with what we're doing and see what happens when we come to a crossroads."

That suited Whittle, who nodded and said, "Fair enough."

They had filled their water vessels and gotten the horses ready to go when Stick took a leather satchel from one of his two canvas bags, unsnapped the catch on the satchel and withdrew a fold of brown paper. It was an original map, something that Stick had sketched during his maiden trip up the Chisholm Trail. Since that journey he had conferred with an assortment of travelers and made numerous revisions to his sketch. For example, the Black Bear River had been erased and redrawn three different times. These improvements notwithstanding, the map was at best a vague representation of the world between central Texas and southern Nebraska, and the cartographer himself sometimes had difficulty interpreting his own creation.

As Stick stood studying the brown paper, Whittle got onto Ben and reminded his partner, "You know, you haven't said yet where you're headed after Caldwell."

"Abilene, Kansas," Stick answered without looking up.

"Oh," Whittle replied, surprised by Stick's forthrightness. "What's next on your map?"

"Should be a range of hills not far from here. The south fork of the Canadian River is about half a day north."

"The Canadian River? I thought we were in America."
Stick folded the map and returned it to his satchel.
"We're in the Indian Nations, Whittle. The Canadian is
just a name. It wanders in from the west and flows into the
Arkansas River."

Whittle frowned and looked away. "I knew that. I was
just checking to see if you knew."

They found the hills, which were low in altitude yet
rugged in character. For more than two hours the pair fought
their way up brush-covered slopes, through mesquite-filled
valleys, around impenetrable briar patches and across the
humped tops of numerous mounds and summits. It was a
trying passage, and as they left the hills behind and returned
to the facile flatness of the plains, Stick remarked, "Glad
that hellish stretch is behind us."

"I'll say," rejoined Whittle. "Might have been easier to
dig a tunnel and ride the horses through."

"Right. We could have used your prospecting trowel."

"Got it right here in my haversack."

They rode through the afternoon and into the last hour
of light before dusk, and were thinking of calling it quits for
the day when they saw a line of treetops stretching diago-
nally across the horizon. The lower portions of the trees
were obscured behind a sharp drop in the land. Stick halted,

studied the trees, then announced proudly, "There it is, the south fork of the Canadian, just like my map predicted."

Whittle was distracted and did not immediately reply. He stared at a fixed point on the horizon. Soon he asked, "What's yonder? Is that a wagon?"

Stick grabbed his telescope and directed the instrument to where Whittle was peering. "Yep. It's a wagon all right, and there's a man on the buckboard picking his toes. A sign on the wagon says 'George Tweed & Company, Purveyor.' I don't see any horses. They must be down by the river."

Whittle looked askance at Stick and wondered, "Did you say, picking his toes?"

"Yep." Stick put away the telescope. "Let's go say hello."

They rode slowly forward, and when the man on the buckboard saw them approaching, he snatched a rifle off the seat beside him and set it across his lap. At the same time he turned toward the trees and called to an unseen companion.

Out of courtesy, and because they didn't want to get shot, Stick and Whittle slowed to an even slower pace than before. A large, powerfully built man emerged from the trees and went to stand at the rear of the wagon.

Stick and Whittle halted approximately thirty yards from the wagon and Stick waved to the two men. The man on the wagon had a rotund figure, a chubby face and bushy sideburns. He had on a straw hat and was about fifty years of age. The standing man was much younger. He was wearing a simple cloth cap, canvas trousers rolled up to his knees and a cotton vest with no shirt. The man on the wagon lifted a hand and gestured for Stick and Whittle to come closer. They did, traveling another fifteen yards before the barefoot man said, "That's close enough. What brings you?"

Stick answered in a peaceable tone, "Just riding along when we saw your wagon. I'm Stick and this is my partner, Whittle. We mean well."

The man on the buckboard eyed the riders warily. Stick was in want of a shave and Whittle was long overdue for new clothes, yet they evidently did not strike the man as dangerous, for he touched the fringed brim of his hat and replied, "Pleased to hear you mean well. George Tweed is my name. That's Cyrus. Hop down if you care to visit."

The riders dismounted. Up until now Whittle had deferred to Stick and let him take the lead, but the instant Whittle's feet hit the ground he strode toward the man on the buckboard, set his hands on his hips and said with aplomb, "Excuse me, Mister Tweed. I can't help but notice. Have you got corns?"

If George Tweed was surprised by the question, he did a fine job of disguising the fact. "Worse than corns, I'm afraid. I've got carbuncles."

Whittle winced sympathetically. "Are they oozing?"

George Tweed nodded. "A little."

"Then you ought to soak your feet in hot, salty water. A friend of mine had oozing carbuncles once. He cured them that way."

The expression on George Tweed's face shifted. He was obviously impressed by the boy's medical acumen. "I appreciate the advice. Fact is, I was fixing to soak just as soon as Cyrus hauled up water and built a fire. We only got our wagon out of the bottom there a few minutes ago."

Stick turned and faced Cyrus. "We've got two thirsty mounts. If you hold up a minute while we undress our horses, I'll go to the river with you and help gather wood."

Cyrus accepted the offer with a nod.

As the travelers removed gear from their horses, George Tweed informed the duo, "Don't mind Cyrus if he don't say much. He ain't got no tongue."

Whittle shot an alarmed look at Cyrus, then averted his eyes when the big man met his gaze.

George Tweed chuckled. "Nothing to be alarmed at. Cyrus still has all his teeth. He can eat."

Whittle blushed awkwardly and concentrated on Ben's saddle pad. After a few seconds he whispered discreetly to Stick, "They appear honest, but that could be an act. I'd better come to the river with you and watch your back."

Stick gave the boy a look that said such precautions were unnecessary. However, Whittle ignored the look, and when the men went to the river, he followed.

As it turned out, George Tweed and his speechless assistant were decent fellows with more or less normal dispositions. When they kindly invited Stick and Whittle to join them for supper, the offer was accepted, and within the hour George Tweed had his fat feet in a tub of salty, hot water and Cyrus had a cauldron of bacon-bean stew hanging over a crackling fire. Mercy and Ben stood near the rear of the wagon, nibbling hay in the company of two gigantic mules. The mules were named At and Et.

Stick could hardly believe his luck. Just as he and Whittle had been running out of supplies they'd met a purveyor with a loaded wagon. Now, for one dollar and a half (Whittle pitched in five dimes) he and his traveling companion owned a dozen pickled eggs, two pounds of beans, a slab of sliced bacon and an almost current issue of the *New York Herald*. The paper, dated May 29, was less than two weeks old! Although a lack of reading light prevented Stick from promptly devouring the news, the prospect of doing so in the near future thrilled him deeply.

There was only one low point in the evening. It came

after supper when Whittle asked George Tweed where he and Cyrus had come from and where they were bound.

"We left Fort Gibson three days ago, heading to Fort Cobb. 'Tain't far. Should be there by noon tomorrow. All them barrels we're hauling are for General Sheridan."

Stick bristled. His change of mood was so abrupt that even the horses and mules were aware of the shift. Mercy snorted, Et brayed and soon George Tweed queried, "You carrying a grudge against Sheridan?"

"Not a personal one," Stick said flatly.

George Tweed stroked his sideburns thoughtfully. "I take it you fought in the war."

"I did."

"What's done is done, I reckon," George Tweed noted philosophically. "It doesn't do much good holding a military man to blame for his duties."

Stick bristled again (no other word for it) and informed the chubby purveyor in a scornful tone, "A man's a man, no matter his calling, and Philip Sheridan is a scoundrel."

George Tweed was startled by Stick's heated outburst. So were Cyrus and Whittle.

Stick saw that the party was shocked, but he didn't care and he continued hotly, "I'm no pansy. I know that war was never meant to be pretty. Even so, fighting is one thing and maliciousness is another. After some of Sheridan's tactics around Petersburg, the man can fry in hell as far as I'm concerned. He will if justice is done."

George Tweed held up his hands and cringed defensively. "You're looking at a businessman here. Sheridan pays his bills when they're due. That's all I know about the general. Frankly, it's all I care to know."

"Business is business," rejoined Whittle. This was the first he'd ever seen of Stick's stormy nature and he was anxious to be done with the subject. So, evidently, was Cyrus, who nodded in mute support of Whittle.

Stick paused to grapple with a private emotion, then sighed and let his anger fall away. It was not his mission to refight the war. He had no need to further besmirch the general.

To everyone's relief — Stick included — this low point in the evening was forgotten moments after George Tweed instructed Cyrus to fetch his medicine bag from the wagon. Cyrus did as he was bid, then George withdrew a brass flask from the bag, unscrewed its silver cap and presented it to Stick in a courtly manner. "If you will, have a nip of this. It's good, store-bought stuff from Sedalla, Missouri."

Stick swigged, grimaced and passed the flask to Cyrus, who swigged, grimaced and passed the flask to Whittle. The boy wasn't the least bit intimidated. After all, he had imbibed bumblebee-bottom extracts and knew a thing or two about corrupting liquids. Or at least he thought he knew before taking an incautious gulp from the flask. First his face contorted and burned red, then he shuddered, froth spewed from his nose and he screamed, "MAN ALIVE!" Shortly after screaming he went bug-eyed. Shortly after that he was unable to discern whether the roar he heard was inside his head or coming from the people he saw swimming in the air around the campfire.

George Tweed chuckled, and retrieved his flask from Whittle's trembling hands. "Those mule-skinners in Sedalla know how to make some wicked whiskey."

SEVEN

STICK AWOKE AT dawn to find that Cyrus had already risen, revived the fire pit and boiled water for coffee. As Stick sat up, the big man smiled and handed him a steaming cup of coffee. He accepted the cup with an appreciative nod. It seemed to Stick that Cyrus was one of those rare individuals who was content with his role in life.

Breakfast was served within the half hour. Twenty minutes after that the two parties had packed their gear, said their adieus and gone their separate ways. Such easy partings were the usual occurrence on the western frontier.

Whittle raced ahead on Ben and waited for Stick and Mercy to join them on the riverbank. The boy was eager to get started, his outlook brightened by the knowledge that he owned stock in twelve pickled eggs. Stick was in a traveling mood as well, although he already entertained notions of stopping soon to read his paper.

The riders held their gear above the waterline and trusted their horses to find the far bank of the river. Ben proved to be a strong swimmer and easily kept abreast of long-legged Mercy. Midway across Whittle called to Stick. "Wonder what happened to Cyrus's tongue."

"How should I know?" Stick was busy watching the shore and holding his rifle over his head.

"I didn't say you should know," Whittle retorted. "I said I wonder. But now that we're on the subject, do you think Comanches got him? I heard they tortured prisoners."

Stick frowned and said nothing. He did not wish to encourage Whittle in such grim speculations — not that the boy's imagination needed any fostering.

They emerged from the river and followed a feeder stream north until they came to a sharp bend where a solitary cottonwood grew on a moss-covered bank. It was the sort of setting Stick was hoping to find. He stopped by the tree and dismounted.

Whittle halted a few feet away and grumbled, "What now?"

Stick was amused by the boy's tone and replied facetiously, "I should have told you before, but I don't like egg whites. I'm going to cut open our dozen and separate the yellows for me."

"Hogwash."

Stick snickered, retrieved his satchel from a pack, took out the newspaper he'd acquired from George Tweed and went to sit with his back against the trunk of the tree.

"So, you're going to read," Whittle observed bitterly. "What am I supposed to do, sit here and wait like a bump on a log?"

Stick grinned and unfolded his paper. "I've got fishing line and hooks. You could catch us lunch."

Whittle shot a murderous look at his irreverent partner, but Stick didn't notice — his attention had already been absorbed by the front page headlines. Whittle dropped from Ben's back, threw his haversack on the ground and sat on the bank with his feet dangling over the stream. He fumed privately for thirty seconds, then said over his shoulder, "I'll pretend I'm fishing. Just holler when you're ready to go."

Stick was thousands of miles away: Letters had arrived in Bombay announcing that the great explorer Doctor Livingston had been found in the interior of Africa. The letters had been mailed from Zanzibar. An account of the expedition would soon be furnished by Mr. Stanley, Commander of the Herald Special Search Corps.

Chief Red Cloud, Red Dog and other Sioux warriors were in Washington to meet President Grant.

One week earlier a tornado had caused immense damage in Missouri. Farms had been demolished, houses were blown down and three unfortunate persons were swept away in their dwellings and drowned.

A fire in Biddeford, Massachusetts, had consumed a law firm, a billiard saloon, an International Telegraph office and Shaw's Opera House.

An equestrian feat had been spoiled in Chicago when

Dexter Park, The California Boy, was thrown from his horse after 198 laps around a seven-eighths-mile-long track. Dexter now lay in a very low state, although the attending physician had some hopes for his eventual recovery.

Stick quit reading and looked up. Whittle was standing over him, trying to bore holes through the paper with his eyes. Stick stiffened and lowered the paper, and Whittle said, "You can stay and memorize your paper. I'm going on."

Stick sighed wearily. The boy had confessed to being ornery on occasion, but Stick had never imagined Whittle could be this irritable. And as if to punctuate the annoying fact, Whittle stomped over to Ben and hopped on the pony's back. "I'll keep an eye peeled for you in Caldwell."

Stick was a patient man, but only to a degree, which had now been surpassed. "Hold it. You're not leaving without me."

Whittle wriggled his nose. "I don't remember making you head of this outfit."

Stick got hot and said, "Thanks for the gratitude. I'm a simple man, Whittle. I don't enjoy many distractions in life, but newspapers are my favorite pastime. A more considerate partner might have let me read in peace."

Whittle hung his head. He was properly admonished. "I'm sorry, Stick. I don't know why I got so fidgety. It just hit me. Anyways, I didn't know you felt so strongly about newspapers."

Still waters run deep was the message in Stick's eyes.

Whittle shifted on Ben and offered sheepishly, "You go ahead and read. I'll sit. Take all the time you need."

Stick snorted, got to his feet, folded his newspaper and returned it to his satchel. "I'm up now. Let's go."

Stick swung onto Mercy and rode forward. Whittle followed a short distance behind, waiting nearly a minute before laughing and telling Stick, "You ought to know I wouldn't have left you. You've got the eggs."

Stick smiled darkly and kept riding.

The two Melvins had been traveling for several hours when they jumped a jackrabbit, which sprang four feet in the air and bounded across the prairie. Whittle reached for his derringer and got off a quick shot. *Bap* went the little gun. Stick snickered and observed, "You were wide by three feet and high by ten."

"It's tricky shooting from a horse," Whittle defended himself. "I scared him though. Look at that bugger run."

"Umhum. I was faster than that when I was your age."

"You were not."

"Sure I was. Rabbit like that, I'd run him down and catch him by the hind legs."

"Stick . . . oh, never mind."

"What?"

"Nothing. It'd be a waste of words arguing with you."

"Durn, my own partner doesn't believe me."

They proceeded northward throughout the long afternoon and reached the main branch of the Canadian River shortly before nightfall. Stick built a small fire and fried a skillet full of bacon. They each ate a pickled egg along with the bacon, then let the fire exhaust itself and retired early.

Whittle had been sleeping for more than an hour when he was awoken by a voice. The boy's eyes blinked open and he sat up. It was Stick, mumbling in his dreams again. Although Whittle had no great desire to eavesdrop on his partner, he would have had to put his hands over his ears to successfully ignore Stick. But Whittle didn't conceive of that option, so he went ahead and eavesdropped. Most of what Stick mumbled was incoherent, and yet the boy repeatedly discerned the word *fire*, the phrase *where are you* and the name *Ezekiel*. Obviously, Stick was having the same distressing dream he'd had the night he and Whittle met.

The longer Whittle sat listening to Stick, the more he grew worried, and he began to wonder if he should wake his partner or leave him be. Meanwhile, Stick continued to moan and mutter inarticulately. Finally, Whittle reached over, tapped Stick on the arm and tentatively suggested,

"Maybe you should wake up." When that didn't work, he tapped harder and spoke louder. "You better wake up." After that failed, he grabbed Stick's shoulders, shook him roughly and cried, "STICK. QUIT DREAMING."

Stick's eyes flew open, and as they did he could feel the Wilderness nightmare receding from his consciousness. His first fully awake thought was, *Whittle is squatting over me*, and he stammered, "Wha wha . . . what are you doing?"

"Just sitting here," answered the boy. "You were mumbling and you didn't sound good, so I woke you up."

Stick drew a breath and exhaled. "I had my dream again. It just won't let me be."

"You all right?"

"I will be."

"Want to tell me about it? Slender Thomas said people should talk about their dreams, especially the bad ones."

Stick lifted up on his elbows. "Slender Thomas?"

"Yep. He knew a lot about dreams." Whittle retreated to his blanket. "According to Slender Thomas everybody has a stranger living inside them and dreams are the thoughts of that stranger. When you speak about your dreams the inside person gets happy and both of you feel better."

"He said that?"

"More or less." Whittle nodded. "Now go on. I bet you haven't told anyone before."

Stick pondered a long while before sighing and beginning the painfully familiar story of his dream, which was virtually the same as the story of what happened at Wilderness. "It was eight years ago, the fifth of May, 1864. I was with my friend Ezekiel. We were back in Virginia after marching south from Gettysburg under Robert E. Lee's command. Ezekiel and I were in A. P. Hill's division. There were sixty-some thousand of us all together and Grant was coming after us with more than a hundred thousand men. It was terribly hot for that time of year and we dug defenses on a patch of high ground near Wilderness Tavern. There was a thicket of woods behind us. Everybody knew a big fight was in the making. Grant had Hancock and Sedgewick with him. Maybe you've never heard those names before, Whittle, but they were fighting men with big reputations, and they were getting tired of chasing Lee. They just wanted to get the war over with and go home, and to do that, they were anxious to crush our army once and for all. Of course, we couldn't allow that to happen . . . so the mood was mighty serious, with everybody sweating for a determined fight."

When Stick paused, Whittle leaned forward. The boy was all ears and could hardly wait for Stick to continue. He did so, saying, "There we were, dug in and waiting for the Yankees to come after us, and soon they started with cannons, trying to soften our lines. After an hour of that,

Hancock threw his whole division at us. All you could hear was the *ka-pow-pow* of muskets. It was insane. You couldn't see for smoke or think for the smell of gunpowder. *Ka-pow. Ka-pow.* It was kill or be killed, and plenty of men were . . . somewheres in the neighborhood of three thousand an hour, if you can believe that. I was loading and shooting at blue shirts, and praying not to get hit, and it was all happening so fast there wasn't time to drink water or hardly breathe. I don't know where the day went, but somehow night came along and both sides stopped to eat a little and sleep a little, and then we all woke up fighting the next day.

"I tell you, Whittle, I was so tired I couldn't think of my own name. It was load and shoot, load and shoot . . . then late on that second day our lines got pushed back into the woods, except you couldn't call them lines because everybody was scattered and mixed in all confused. Hancock kept coming, and he would've broken us if Longstreet hadn't showed at the last minute. God bless Longstreet. They say he hesitated at Gettysburg, but he was right on time at Wilderness. He sure saved us from going under. Longstreet had odd luck, though, because later he was accidentally shot by one of his own men. By then it was night and the woods were so thick with soldiers you couldn't tell who was a Yankee and who wasn't, so nobody was blamed. Anyway, the guns kept blasting and wounded men were screaming, and . . . well . . ." Stick's voice trailed off and sank into silence.

"Well what?" Whittle prompted after a moment.

Stick drew a breath and resumed his tale. "Well, just when you thought it could not get any worse, the Devil himself came along and set the woods afire. There were only a few flames at first, but they kept jumping from tree to tree and the next anyone knew the woods were burning all around us and we were penned in. There was no place to run for fear of stumbling into Yankees. It was the same for them too, all dark and smoky, and nobody could see to help the wounded. Men were screaming and shooting. It was hell and out of nowhere I heard Ezekiel holler, 'I've been hit. Melvin, lend a hand.' I tried to find him, but I couldn't see, so I hollered, 'Where are you, Ezekiel?' and he answered, 'I'm here. Help me.' When I turned to where I thought he was, I felt a hot streak across my forehead, and then I was blind with blood in my face . . . and Ezekiel was still calling, 'Melvin, I've been hit. It's bad.' I must have passed out, because the next thing I knew it was morning and I was in a wagon of wounded headed for Fredericksburg. I don't know if you'd call it luck, but Ezekiel was in the wagon too. He was missing half a shoulder and had been shot in the stomach. It wasn't good luck — that's for sure. He was alive, but he didn't know who I was, or who he was for that matter. I couldn't take looking at his shoulder, so I put my jacket around him. After that I must've passed out again because all I remember is waking up in Chancellorsville and Ezekiel wasn't on the wagon anymore. I guess he died and somebody hauled him away." Stick fell silent for a spell, then added, "So that's the dream I keep having. Over and over . . . always the same."

Whittle stared at Stick for a long time, waiting until he was sure his partner had nothing more to say, then offered in a caring, sympathetic tone, "That's a rough tale, Stick, and I've heard plenty of rough ones. Fact is, my life hasn't been a bed of roses. I never knew my ma or pa. They dropped me off with Miss Prescott and disappeared. Not that I give an honest hoot. Who needs parents? But forget that — I'm just telling you that I'm qualified for judging sad stories, and you've got one."

"Hmph."

"You did right, sharing it with me, Stick. I bet the person inside of you feels better already."

"I feel tired right now. That's all I know."

"Get some sleep," said Whittle. "Things'll look better in the morning. Thanks for telling me what happened to you."

Stick lay back on his bedroll and sighed. "Yeah. Thanks for listening."

"Sure. That's what partners are for."

EIGHT

THE NEXT MORNING Stick and Whittle both awoke in somber moods, feeling listless and unambitious. Perhaps their spirits were oppressed by the malingering weight of Stick's Wilderness dream, or maybe they were just out of get-up-and-go. Whatever the case, neither Melvin had any enthusiasm for rising and getting on with the day. Indeed, they were still in supine positions twenty minutes after the sun had made its daily debut. Strange. Even the horses had a lazy look about them as they grazed the sweet grass along the riverbank.

Eventually, Stick stirred from his bedroll, pulled on his boots and declared that he wasn't going anywhere until after he had shaved. That was fine with Whittle, who yawned and covered his face with a corner of his blanket. Stick built a fire, put on a pot of water and fetched soap and a razor from his packs. When the water was hot, he barbered his stubbly face. Inspired by the hygienic activity, Whittle sat up and wondered, "Say, Stick, mind if I borrow your soap?"

Stick gave his partner a sideways look. "Why? You planning to shave your mustache?"

"No." Whittle shot a hurt look at Stick, then added with a shrug, "I thought I might bathe in the river, maybe give my clothes a wash. I've been noticing an odd smell lately. I think it might be me."

Stick grinned. "Please, take the soap."

After Stick was done shaving, he poured fresh water in the pot, added a measure of coffee, returned the pot to the fire, retrieved his *New York Herald* and perused a story headlined "Love And Jealousy." It was a lurid tale about a husband who stabbed his wife, her paramour and himself — it had all the elements of an intriguing read — and yet for some reason the story failed to hold Stick's attention. He looked at another piece titled "Struck With a Club." Inexplicably, this classic crime story also failed to interest Stick. Hmm. It took him a moment to realize it, but he simply wasn't in a mood for reading this morning. He closed the paper, poured himself a cup of coffee and sat back to think about life. He wasn't more than three thoughts along when he heard Whittle call from down by the river, "Hey, Stick."

"Yeah?" Stick answered over his shoulder.

"There's a huge snapping turtle in a pool here. Want to help me catch him?"

"Better leave that snapper alone if you're naked, Whittle. He'll make a girl out of you in a jiffy."

"Ha. Ha. That's very funny."

"Come on and get dressed now. The day is slipping by and there's plenty of ground ahead of us."

Whittle soon appeared by the campfire wearing his wet clothes. "Thanks for the loan," he said, tossing the wet bar of soap to Stick and sitting to yank on his boots. His long brown hair had been brushed back with his fingers and was exposed to the world. After the last brouhaha with his derby, he had no intentions of putting on a hat until his hair was thoroughly dry. He got both boots on, then sighed, gazed quizzically at Stick and said, "So, I was wondering something that you might tell me."

"Were you?"

"Yep."

"What?"

"Your jacket, the one you put around Ezekiel, did you ever get it back?"

Stick stiffened slightly, and at the same time, gave Whittle a look of begrudging admiration. How had the boy managed to come up with that question? Of all the private matters Stick did not wish to share, Whittle had struck at his most guarded. Still, he had to give the boy credit. "You're quite a detective. I hear the Pinkerton Agency is hiring."

"So, I was right?"

"Yes," Stick reluctantly confirmed. "I never got my jacket back . . . and that caused a lot of problems later on."

Whittle nodded. "It had your papers in it, didn't it?"

Stick lowered his head and pondered the ground for nearly a minute. Finally he looked up and said, "From when the bullet hit me, I had a concussion that kept me in the hospital for a week. By the time I recovered and was able to prove who I was, mistakes had been made and certain people had the wrong information about my condition. They, ah . . . were confused about my existence."

Whittle got to his feet and shook out his blanket. "They thought you were dead?"

"Some did." Stick stood and started organizing his gear.

"Who? Anybody special?"

Stick stiffened and shot a withering look at his partner.

Whittle lowered his gaze and concentrated on folding his blanket. Although Stick's reaction had done more to inflame his curiosity than diminish it, Whittle understood that now was not the time to press the matter. He figured he'd wait and ask questions later.

They'd been riding five hours and were halfway between the Canadian River and the Red Fork of the Arkansas when Stick halted on the plain and waited for Whittle to draw up beside him. "What?" asked the boy, and Stick replied, "There's two people ahead of us. They were walking before, but they just sat down."

"Where?"

"Straight on a thousand yards."

The boy held a hand up to shield the sun from his eyes and squinted. "Those huddled shapes? That what you're talking about?"

"Yep. Indians."

"Indians!" Whittle's voice cracked with excitement. "Are you sure? Wow. I thought I'd never."

Stick shot a warning look at Whittle. "Calm down."

"Sorry. What are they doing?"

"Waiting to see what we do, I believe."

"It could be a trap."

"Shush," said Stick, "and quit fidgeting so much. You'll fall off your pony."

"No I won't." Whittle bit his bottom lip and struggled to contain himself.

Stick reached slowly for his telescope and lifted it to an eye. He soon reported, "It's an old man and a girl."

"Indians, right?" Whittle wondered.

"Yes. Maybe Cheyenne." Stick put away his telescope. "Come on. Ride slowly beside me. We don't want to alarm them."

Whittle agreed with a nod and continued to bite his bottom lip as they rode forward. They halted fifty yards from the seated pair and Stick held up his right hand, palm outward. For a moment no one moved. After a brief spell the girl stood and faced the riders. Again, no one moved, except for Whittle, who trembled with excitement.

The girl wore beaded moccasins, a deerskin skirt fringed below her knees and a plain white blouse. A pair of raven-black braids dangled to her waist and she viewed the world through dark, saucer-shaped eyes nestled above plump, rounded cheeks buttoned together by a narrow ridged nose. She was one of the prettiest, most enthralling females Whittle had ever seen. With a thrust of will he tore his gaze from the girl and looked at the man, who was as fascinating as the girl was beautiful. The old Indian had a large, impassive face and a shock of cloud-white hair that fell past both shoulders. On his head was a woven band. A hawk feather stood erect at the back of his head. He was wearing a sleeveless shirt made of tanned hides, and coarse canvas pants tied at the waist with rope. A quiver of arrows hung from his left shoulder and a bow rested across his lap. On the ground behind the old man lay a bundle of belongings wrapped in animal skins.

After remaining immobile for thirty seconds or so, the girl raised her right hand and held it palm outward to Stick. It was the signal he'd been waiting for and he dropped his hand. The girl dropped her hand, said something to the man in a language that neither Stick nor Whittle understood, waited for the man's response, then gestured for the riders to dismount and approach on foot.

They stopped ten yards from the girl and the man. Stick removed his sombrero and said, "Hello. We come in peace."

To his and Whittle's astonishment the girl replied, "We thought you were lost, white men. What do you want?"

Stick took a moment to compose his reply. As it was, he did not have to worry about Whittle speaking before him. The boy was wide-eyed and mute with wonder. Soon Stick answered, "We saw you here with no horses. We came to offer help."

The girl translated for the old man. He stared at Stick and considered for a few seconds, then said something to the girl, who turned and informed Stick, "We are walking home. We do not need your help."

Stick took a step backwards. He had never been the type to thrust himself on strangers, and he was particularly sensitive toward this native pair. However, as Stick drew back, Whittle stepped forward, doffing his derby and bowing to the girl. He had managed to untie his tongue. "We've got pickled chicken eggs to spare. Would you like one? They're mighty tasty with salt."

The girl eyed Whittle with an expression that was

virtually impossible to interpret. Perhaps there was a hint of amusement in her look, or maybe she was surprised by the offer. At any rate, she replied, "My grandfather is fond of chicken eggs."

Whittle beamed at the girl, and without taking his eyes off her, reached to tug Stick's arm. "Quick, fetch the eggs."

Stick frowned. He didn't appreciate the boy ordering him around in front of strangers. Even so, he approved of Whittle's impulse to share and turned to obey the command. The girl sat down beside her grandfather, and Whittle, like a bear cub drawn to honey, settled on the ground across from the girl. The old man peered at Whittle and made a guttural sound in his throat. The girl said something and looked down. Stick rejoined the group, sat by Whittle and handed two eggs to each person. After a pouch of salt was passed around, everyone ate in silence. Soon the eggs were history, yet the silence lingered . . . until Whittle leapt to his feet and dashed to where Ben was standing with Mercy. He grabbed his canteen, dashed back to the gathering and held the container out to the girl. "Want some water from the Canadian River? It's warm, but it's clean."

The girl accepted the canteen with a dip of her head. "This is nām shǐm´, my grandfather. We are Tsǐs tsǐs´ tǎs, which you call Cheyenne."

The boy put a hand on his chest. "I'm Whittle. My partner's name is Stick. We're Americans."

The old man grunted and suddenly Whittle was aware of unfathomably dark eyes examining him from head to toe. Whittle felt himself gripped and held in place by an invisible power. He could not have moved an inch if he tried and he was immensely thankful he had no secrets to hide. After a lengthy moment the old man turned and spoke to the girl. She translated for Whittle, "My grandfather wants to know if you stole your pony from a Comanche."

Whittle glanced quickly at Stick and at the old man, and hesitated. He did not know whether the question had been issued as a challenge or out of simple curiosity. Not knowing how else to respond, he answered honestly, "I bought that pony from a man in Louisiana."

Again, the old man spoke to the girl, and she translated, "My grandfather admires your pony. He says if you feed plums to your pony it will never abandon you."

An involuntary moan escaped from Whittle. It was a happy moan. The old Indian had looked into the boy from Chicago and deemed him worthy of horse wisdom. Whittle bowed humbly and said, "His name is Ben."

"Ben," the old man repeated. He understood.

Whittle was thrilled through and through. He peeked at

the girl out of the corner of his eye and — in a classic case of wishful thinking — determined that his status had risen in her eyes. It was all too much for Whittle, who fell suddenly silent in thought. The subsequent pause allowed Stick to finally enter the conversation. He addressed the girl, saying, "My compliments on your English. You speak well."

"I learned from the chaplain at Fort Dodge," she replied modestly.

"You lived at Fort Dodge?" asked Stick. He did not doubt the girl; he was curious.

"Yes. From when I was six years old until I was nine."

Suddenly the old man grunted. He had recognized the words for Fort Dodge and was evidently bitter about what the words represented. Obviously, Stick reflected, Fort Dodge reminded the old Cheyenne warrior of uniformed soldiers. Stick made eye contact with the old man and grew solemn with sympathy. His habit of reading newspapers had left him shamefully aware of numerous injustices inflicted upon the Cheyenne by uniformed men in the past dozen years. It was conceivable that the old man had been present at the Sand Creek massacre — perhaps the single most barbaric event in United States history. Stick recalled that upwards of a hundred (some reports say twice that many or more) defenseless women and children had been slain at Sand Creek by a Colorado militia commanded by a retired Protestant minister. And in an added ugliness to the horror, almost all of the victims were mutilated and scalped. Ah, the hypocrisy of man. How morally decrepit was it possible to be? The mere thought of Sand Creek made Stick embarrassed to be human. As far as he was concerned, the old man had every right to be bitter. So did the girl.

Perhaps it was the consciousness of things past, or maybe it was just time to go, yet for whatever reason, the old man eyed the girl and they both stood. The man bent to pick up their bundle and hoisted it on his back. Although old, he was not feeble. The girl acknowledged Stick with a look, then said to Whittle, "Thank you for sharing food with us. I am Brings the Rain. My grandfather is called Talking Rock."

A pang of anxiety shot through Whittle and he jumped to his feet, desperate to delay the pair's departure, if only for a few moments. "So where is your home?"

Brings the Rain glanced at her grandfather, who had already begun to walk away, then informed Whittle, "We are going beyond the Salt Plains, to the place where Bear Creek meets the Cimarron River. My grandfather was born there. He returns to his beginning where he will sing his Death-song."

Whittle did not understand. "Death-song?"

Brings the Rain dropped her eyes. "It is the song one sings before one never sings again."

"Oh," Whittle said sadly, waiting until Brings the Rain lifted her eyes before asking, "Is Bear Creek far?"

Brings the Rain's reply was cryptic. "What is near?"

Whittle removed his hat, held it over his heart and could not resist saying, "You are near."

Something subtle shifted in Brings the Rain's face and she looked deep into Whittle's eyes. Much like what had happened with Talking Rock, the boy was rendered immobile, only now he was held tenderly captive instead of firmly gripped. For several timeless seconds the girl held the boy in place, and then she gifted him with a sweet, warm smile. Whittle shuddered as if he'd been shot with an arrow and watched as Brings the Rain turned and hurried to catch up with her grandfather.

NINE

STICK AND WHITTLE stood side by side, watching silently as Talking Rock and Brings the Rain grew smaller and smaller in the distance. When the receding figures finally shrank from view, Whittle sighed wistfully and said, "I don't know if you noticed, Stick, but Brings the Rain smiled at me before she left."

"I saw that. She gave you a sweet good-bye."

"It will be a long while before I forget her."

"I know the feeling."

"Man alive."

"Come on. Standing isn't getting us anywhere."

The travelers got on their horses and headed north. A good six hours of light remained in the day. Although the sun seemed determined to cook them, they made good progress over the broad, flat plains.

They crossed the Red Fork of the Arkansas River at dusk, then followed one of its tributaries for several hundred yards and pitched camp in a copse of dwarf conifers growing at the rocky base of an elevated plateau. Actually, Stick did all the pitching while Whittle sat with his arms around his knees and vaguely watched a pumpkin-colored crescent moon rise above the treetops.

By the time night fell over the land, Stick had a pot of bacon-bean stew simmering over a hissing, sap-saturated bed of evergreen limbs. After giving oats to Mercy and Ben, he relieved himself in the woods, then settled down across from Whittle. The boy was still musing at the moon and gave no sign that he was aware of Stick's presence. Whatever Whittle was thinking, it was obviously important and far away. Stick sat back, slipped his bowie knife from its sheath and began trimming his fingernails. He understood the need for inner reflection and wished to afford the boy his privacy. Meanwhile the musical little fire hissed, popped, snapped and whistled in the night.

Stick completed his manicure, waited another ten minutes or so, then picked up his spoon and tasted the bacon-bean stew. Too much salt. It needed pepper. No matter. He ate it anyway. When he was done he set his bowl on the ground and looked at the boy, who was still mooning. In the five days since they had met, Stick had never seen Whittle so thoughtful and withdrawn — at least not for such a sustained length of time — and in a funny way the boy's enduring silence made him nervous. Finally, Stick determined that enough was enough and attempted to evoke a word from his partner. "In case you haven't noticed," he said to the boy, "your grub is ready to eat. Or maybe you gave up eating when you quit talking."

Whittle acknowledged Stick with a vacuous look, yet did not speak. He was not quite there.

Stick washed his meal down with a gulp of water, wiped his mouth with the heel of a hand and tried again to engage his ruminant partner. "Something is troubling you. I can't imagine what it is, but you listened me out when I talked about my dream and I'll do the same for you now . . . if you're inclined to share your thoughts."

Whittle slowly came to life, unwrapping his arms from his knees and lowering his gaze from the moon. "That map of yours, does it show Bear Creek?"

Stick suppressed a smile. Now he knew what was bothering Whittle: The boy was pining for Brings the Rain. "No," Stick answered empathetically. "Bear Creek isn't on my map, but the Salt Plains are clearly marked. They're west of here, a bit to the north."

Whittle made a mental note of the information and informed Stick, "I'm worried about Brings the Rain. What will she do after Talking Rock sings his Death-song?"

Stick rubbed his chin and allowed, "That's hard to say, but I suspect she'll go back to her people . . . if she has any. She probably does somewhere."

Whittle nodded, hesitated a moment, then said, "I want to ask you a question that's only a question."

"Oh. A hypothetical inquiry."

"Quit with the big words, Stick. It's a question for thinking about. Okay?"

"Sure. Go ahead, ask away."

Whittle threw a quick glance at the moon before gazing at Stick and wondering aloud, "Say I went looking for Brings the Rain. You think I'd have any chance of finding her?"

Stick weighed the question against the backdrop of his own experience. Of course, Whittle's nascent infatuation for the Cheyenne girl did not warrant comparison with his eight-year search for Evelyn Laroue, and yet there were mutual elements of yearning in both situations. Stick was wise enough to answer delicately. "You might find her, if you got lucky, but it would take some serious looking."

"Might, unh? That doesn't tell me much."

"Truth is, there's no way to know until you try," Stick noted philosophically, adding, "One thing to consider: if Talking Rock is going to sing his Death-song, I would guess it's a private affair. Maybe he and Brings the Rain don't want to be found."

"Yeah, maybe."

"Besides . . . Indian camps are never easy to find."

Whittle studied Stick thoughtfully, then glanced again

at the moon and heaved a sigh. "Like I said before, it was only a question."

"Right."

Whittle reached for his wooden bowl and dolloped out a sizeable scoop of stew. "So, have you ever loved a girl?"

Stick stiffened slightly. Where did the boy come up with these questions? Stick forced himself to relax and affected a casual tone, "That's only natural."

Whittle filled his spoon and held it in front of his mouth. "What happened? Do you love her still?"

Stick furrowed his brow. A moment ago he'd been trying to draw the boy out of his shell, but now the reverse was true, and he replied defensively, "Don't you think that's getting into personal terrain?"

"I don't know. I was asking." The boy shoved the contents of the spoon in his mouth, chewed and swallowed.

Stick studied the fire for several seconds, then — somewhat to his own surprise — offered forthrightly, "I haven't seen her for quite some time, but the answer is yes, I still love her."

"Interesting. What's her name?"

Stick pretended not to hear.

Whittle filled his spoon and again paused with it in front of his mouth. "You're not ashamed of her, are you?"

Stick bristled. "No. And it's rude to even suggest that."

"Sorry," Whittle said sheepishly. He could see that he had hit a sore spot with Stick, and that made him even more curious than before. Although Whittle knew that he risked further rebuke for pressing the subject, he plowed ahead anyway. "This girl that you still love, does she . . . well, does this have anything to do with the jacket you put around Ezekiel?"

Stick winced. The boy had a knack for poignant inquiries. "Not much gets past you, does it?"

"It depends," said Whittle. "Sometimes I'm pretty smart."

Stick shook his head, ruing his luck in hooking up with such a pertinacious partner. He shot a look at the boy that was so complex it could not be described or comprehended. However, Whittle derived his own meaning from the look, and combining that with the information he had, was able to extrapolate, "So, the girl you love thinks you're dead. It must be rough."

Stick made a sound that was half groan and half growl.

Whittle resumed eating and did not speak until after his bowl was empty. He set it aside with his spoon, burped and advised his reluctant partner, "You might as well tell me her name, Stick. I'm going to get it out of you eventually."

"Grr. If you must know, it's Evelyn."

"Ha. That's a pretty name. Describe her for me."

Stick pulled off a boot and grabbed the heel of its mate. "Been a long day. I'm turning in."

"Ah. Come on. Please," Whittle cajoled. "Tell me something. What color is Evelyn's hair?"

In some instances physical expression speaks louder than words. This was one of those instances. Stick yanked off his remaining boot, sprawled out his bedroll, pillowed his head upon his saddle and closed his eyes. It took him awhile, but Whittle eventually got the message, whereupon he straightened out his blanket and lay down.

Soon, way out on the tableland above the campers, a clan of coyotes made their doleful presence known. Coyotes are chronic complainers. They love to assemble in discordant choirs and sing awful, eerie, mournful songs. Such was certainly the case with this clan: Oh, what a ruckus they made. It went on and on and might have lasted all night if not for the intervening howl of a prowling wolf. The coyotes fell silent when the great predator spoke. They revered their lupine cousin. He would eat them if they did not.

Stick was almost asleep when Whittle called to him, "Remind me tomorrow to look for wild plums."

"Hmm."

"Don't forget. It's important."

"Okay."

"Thanks. I want Ben to be happy." Whittle was quiet for a brief while, and Stick was almost asleep again when the boy asked, "This morning, what you said about running down a jackrabbit, you were joshing, right?"

"Yeah."

"I thought so."

"Shush."

"Sorry. Good night." Whittle paused for another brief while then chuckled and added, "Don't let the bedbugs bite."

Stick envisioned digging a hole and burying the boy, but it was only a fantasy, not to be acted upon.

They awoke at first light, ate an egg each for breakfast (that was it for their dozen) and walked their horses along the bluff wall until they found a narrow, winding animal trail that appeared to zigzag upward. It did, and soon they were standing with their mounts looking north across the elevated tableland. A muted brown and green plain stretched out before them like a sheet of monotonous eternity. For mile after mile there was nothing to see but the desolate, windswept hint of an imagined horizon. The world was a haven for gophers, grasshoppers, tumbleweeds and nothing else.

As Stick remarked upon gaining the saddle, "Only one thing to do with this country. That's cross it."

Whittle swung onto Ben and told his pony, "It doesn't look promising. You might have to wait a few days on those plums. Now giddy-up."

During the course of the day's journey Stick veered slightly east from a due northerly tack. That evening they reached the banks of the Black Bear River, where Whittle searched for wild plums while Stick built a fire and cooked supper. Sadly, the boy's search was in vain. Perhaps somebody should have told him that even if he found a plum tree, its fruit would not be ripe until August. The thought crossed Stick's mind, but what with one thing and another, he never mentioned the fact to Whittle.

They moved on in the morning, rode hard for eight hours, and early that afternoon, crossed the Nescutunga River, which some people called the Salt. At this point, for all practical purposes, Stick and Whittle had passed safely through the territory known as the Indian Nations. Two hours after crossing the Nescutunga, just as Stick had planned, the travelers made contact with the previously avoided Chisholm Trail. They followed the well-worn track until night overtook them, then pitched camp in a shallow depression near the side of the popular route. They were approximately ten miles south of Caldwell, Kansas, and a first-quarter moon hung in the sky above the two Melvins. They had been partners now for a week.

TEN

IT WAS LATE morning when Stick and Whittle halted on the outskirts of Caldwell and paused to survey the place before entering. It had a main street, a general store, a hotel, two flophouses, three saloons, a blacksmith's forge, a livery stable, an undertaker's shop and a dozen private homes, yet it was too newly invented and rough around the edges to qualify as an actual town. Better to call it a frontier trading post.

Although Caldwell had a semi-permanent population of nearly one hundred people, it was without a mayor or a marshal, and was subject to a wide array of immoral influences. There were, of course, a few trustworthy, hard-working folks in Caldwell, but they represented a small minority amongst a larger populace drawn from the ranks of itinerant cardsharps, sporting Delilahs, mustachioed gunslingers, smooth-talking con artists, pipedream promoters, hardbitten drunks, brawny opportunists and aimless drifters. The cattlemen that rode the Chisholm Trail and often lost or spent their dollars in Caldwell rather aptly referred to the place as The Border Queen. It was not the sort of place one took one's mother.

It was with a mixture of dismay and droll fascination that Stick and Whittle observed the scene. Near the south end of the main street where the travelers sat on their horses, a man in a plaid suit slept under a wagon next to a pig. Further down the street a disheveled individual in baggy pajamas stumbled from the side door of a building and upchucked in an alley. Across the way a little girl with red pigtails threw a rock at a mangy dog and a portly old man called to someone in a second-floor window. A woman wearing a bonnet stuck her head from the window and shouted to the man, "Henry Lewis, go back to Arkansas and die." Then the window slammed shut, the man in the pajamas passed out in the alley and the little girl threw another rock at the dog.

Stick had seen enough to size up the situation. "All right, Whittle, here's the plan. First, we secure a room in the hotel and sign up for an early supper. Then we take Ben and Mercy to the stable and pay premium keep. They deserve the best after hauling us here from Texas. When that's done, we'll go shopping, *together*, and after that we go back to our room and keep a low profile."

"Wow," Whittle exclaimed sarcastically. "You worked that out by yourself. Didn't even need my opinion."

Stick was not in a jocular mood. "Listen, Whittle, I've come too far in the world to get waylaid by some stranger in a two-bit place like this. If it's town excitement you want, wait until we get to Wichita City. That's only two days from here. Meanwhile, we steer clear of trouble here in Caldwell."

Whittle agreed with a nod. "All I want to do is buy some plums and a bag of licorice. Now let's go, and don't worry so much, Stick. I'm eyes in the back of your head."

Stick smirked and rode forward on Mercy.

There was nothing fancy about the hotel or its name. It was simply called "Hotel." However, the beds in the rooms had horsehair mattresses covered in clean sheets, the locks on the doors were solid and the two-dollar-a-night rate suited Stick. For an extra dollar he arranged for two tubs of hot water to be waiting in a curtained area behind the kitchen at four o'clock. Whittle thought the second tub was unnecessary, explaining that he'd bathed only two days before, but Stick insisted on treating, saying, "Never hurts to get too clean."

They had hauled all their gear up to the second-floor room and had been sitting around for five minutes when Stick tossed his bowie knife on the bed beside his rifle case, cleared his throat and said to Whittle, "I believe I mentioned that I'd recently quit my job before we met. Anyhow, I did, which puts me flush with cash for basics . . . so I plan to pay for everything while we're in Caldwell."

A part of Whittle (the orphan part that had survived on the tough streets of Chicago) urged him to keep his mouth shut and take what came his way, and yet another, better part of the boy overrode that initial urge and prompted him to reply, "Thanks for the offer, but I've still got fourteen dollars. I'll kick in my share."

Stick smiled, pleased by Whittle's show of good character. "All right," he told the boy, "you buy breakfast tomorrow. In the meantime, except for that derby, you're in painful need of a new outfit and I intend to purchase you one. Boots, pants, shirt, socks . . . the whole bit."

Whittle's mouth fell open and he stared at Stick as if suddenly confronted by a strange phenomenon. Indeed, throughout his sixteen years of earthly existence he had rarely encountered generosity and was thus unfamiliar with the feelings that now welled up within him. It almost goes without saying that he was unpracticed at expressing his gratitude, yet that did not stop him from trying. He removed his black bowler and bowed. "Only two people have ever been nice to me before — Slender Thomas and Miss Prescott. One of them is dead and the other was nice to everybody she knew. Anyways . . . thank you." Whittle drew himself erect and returned his derby to his head. "If you ever catch me speaking poorly of you, remind me that I'm an idiot."

"I'll do that," Stick replied with a chuckle. "Now come on. Our belongings are safe in here. Let's settle the horses and go shopping."

"You're backing up if you're waiting for me."

Caldwell's only livery stable was run by a young man named Purcell Washington. Purcell wasn't much of a conversationalist, but he had an honest face and a gentle manner, and Stick and Whittle felt comfortable leaving their horses in his care. Across the street from the stable was Beale's General Store. It was owned and operated by Floyd and Franklin Beale, two brothers from Quincy, Illinois. Outside of the store was an awning and a wooden sidewalk. The sidewalk was narrow and short, but it was solidly built and suggested that the Beale brothers intended to grow roots in Caldwell. Their business plan was simple: Carry a wide variety of items and sell them at fair, frontier-trading-post prices. If you weren't looking for baubles or the latest in fashion, Beale's General Store was an excellent place to shop.

Franklin Beale had no trouble locating undershorts, canvas pants, a cotton shirt and socks to fit Whittle, but he had to rummage in a back room for fifteen minutes before finding a pair of size seven boots to fit the boy. It was well worth the wait. The boots were tanned leather, with padded soles, hand-stitched eyelets for lacing and inch-thick heels. Whittle was utterly delighted and readily agreed with

Franklin's suggestions that they dispose of the old pair. When Franklin stepped out back to toss the derelict boots onto a trash heap, Whittle transferred his derringer from the hip pocket of his old pants to the inner cuff of his new left boot.

The whole while Stick lingered near the front of the store feigning interest in a box of nails. He was actually keeping a wary eye on two gruff-looking customers that Floyd was attending. The suspicious men had placed a keg of gunpowder and three dozen boxes of bullets on the counter, then proceeded to stack several cases of canned corn and beef jerky next to the ammunition. One of the men had an ivory-handled Colt .45 tucked in his belt.

Franklin wrapped Whittle's new pants, shirt and underwear in brown paper and tied the package with a string. Clutching his bundle excitedly, Whittle hurried toward the front of the store to join Stick. He was halfway there when he accidentally brushed against one of the tough guys and dropped his package. "Excuse me," he offered, bending to pick up his new clothes.

"What's the matter, Runt? Can't you see?"

"Of course I can see," Whittle replied bluntly. He didn't like being called Runt. "You stepped out while I was going by. It wasn't my fault."

The man sneered menacingly at Whittle. "I reckon you bumped into me on purpose."

"You reckon wrong, Mister. It was an accident."

"You want to see an accident? Watch this," said the man, and as he spoke he backhanded Whittle across the face, knocking the stunned youngster to the floor.

In less time than it takes to say Caldwell, Kansas, Stick stepped forward and yanked the offending man's arms behind his back. Furious, he lifted upward on the man's wrists and snarled, "Only a rotten coward would slap a kid."

The words were hardly out of Stick's mouth when he felt a blunt point of steel touch the back of his head. A voice said, "You're dead when I pull the trigger." The voice was accented by the sound of a Colt hammer drawing back.

A heavy silence fell over the store. No one moved and no one spoke. You could have heard a mouse sigh.

Whittle broke the silence. He had rolled from his back to his stomach and was reaching upward with his right arm. His derringer was in his hand and the barrel of the pistol was pointed into the groin of the man holding the Colt against Stick's head. Whittle cocked the hammer and said, "Mister, if you don't lower your gun and step away from my partner, you're going to be speaking with a squeaky voice for the rest of your life."

The tough guys glared down at Whittle, then the man that Stick was holding advised his companion, "He appears determined, Curtis. I'd step back if I were you."

"I'll count to three," Whittle warned, yet before he could say one, Franklin Beale emerged from behind the counter with a double-barreled shotgun in his hands and commanded, "You with the Colt, drop it. Son, withdraw your pistol. Sir, release that man's arms and step back. Now everybody do what I said."

Since there was no reason to imagine that Franklin's shotgun was not loaded, everyone did just as Franklin instructed. Then the angry shopkeeper told the two rough customers, "You fellows got what you came for. I want you to settle your bill with Floyd and get out of here."

Before obeying Franklin's command, the man named Curtis shot a withering look at Stick and warned, "You got lucky this time, but it won't be that way if I see you again."

Stick met the man's gaze and did not say a word. There was no need to speak; his expression stated clearly that he thought Curtis was a petty blowhard. Stick waited until the man turned to join his cohort at the counter, then peered proudly at Whittle and said, "Thanks, partner. That was some brave doing."

Whittle picked up his package and stood. "It was nothing. I'm just relieved he didn't call my bluff."

"Bluff?"

"Yeah." Whittle shrugged. "I never reloaded after taking a crack at that rabbit the other day."

Stick shook his head. "Durn, boy, you've got gumption with a capital G."

Whittle grinned. "I'll have style too, soon as I take my bath and get into these new duds."

Later that evening the two Melvins settled upon the bench in their room and watched as the light faded from the skies over Caldwell. They'd eaten a good meal and were clean from head to toe. Although Whittle had not found any plums for Ben, he had procured a bag of licorice drops. "Here," he said, presenting the bag to Stick. "They're for both of us."

Stick plucked a drop from the bag and popped it into his mouth. But for the lack of a current newspaper, he would have been perfectly content.

Whittle, on the other hand, was more than content. He put two licorice drops into his mouth, sighed and declared, "This is great, sitting here in a new outfit . . . full of dumplings and gravy potatoes. Wish I had a good purpose."

"How do you mean?"

"Just as I say," Whittle replied. "Except for following you to Abilene, I don't have a purpose. I haven't had one since Slender Thomas passed over."

"What did you have then . . . before he went?"

Whittle popped another licorice drop into his mouth.

"Well, mostly taking care of Slender Thomas. Anyhow . . . that was then. Nowadays I got a funny need in me to do right somewhere."

"Not sure I follow what you're saying."

Whittle hesitated. It was apparent that something was bothering him — some memory. Reluctantly, he said, "It's too hard to explain. Bascially, I owe the world a favor."

"Why? You can tell me."

"Maybe I will some day. Maybe not."

Stick rubbed his clean-shaven face and wondered what the boy was hiding, or thinking, or whatever.

Whittle decided it was time to turn the conversation around. "So, Stick, how about you? You got a purpose?"

Stick sucked ponderously on his licorice drop. After a moment he swallowed and said, "Yes and no. I had a purpose for the longest time, but it's been fading on me lately."

"I think I know what it was. You were trying to find Evelyn and straighten out that you aren't dead."

Stick made a noise in his throat. It was part laugh and part groan. It was a sad sound. "You're right again, Whittle. I've been looking for the past eight years . . . and let me say, it's hard hoping in vain for that long. It wears a man down."

Whittle shifted self-consciously on the bench. After all that Stick had done for him, he had callously reminded his friend of woeful matters. The boy got up and went to the window, where he stood looking out for a silent spell. Eventually he turned and asked his partner, "You ever hear the saying, the dark hour comes right before the dawn?"

"I've heard it. Why?"

"Just do me a favor and keep it in mind. Okay? I'm not saying Evelyn will show up tomorrow or anything . . . but if you've been hoping this long, you might as well hope a little longer."

Stick wrinkled his brow and shrugged. "I probably will, out of habit."

"Good," said Whittle. "Now I've got a question for you. And don't ask what kind. It's just a question."

"Shoot."

"In your opinion, should I shave my mustache or keep it?"

"Keep it."

A broad smile broke over Whittle's face. "Thanks, partner, that was the opinion I wanted."

ELEVEN

STICK AWOKE BEFORE dawn and bolted upright in the hotel bed. He had dreamed of Wilderness again, yet for the first time he could recall, only a portion of the nightmare had haunted him. Granted, he had dreamed the most horrifying portion containing scenes from the burning woods; still, he was encouraged. At this point, after eight years of intermittent visitations, any change in the overall pattern was promising. Stick glanced over at Whittle, asleep in bed, and wondered how much credit to give the boy. After all, without Whittle's pestering he would never have articulated the dream, and — if this be true — given voice to the stranger living inside of him. Was it possible that he had made that stranger happy and somehow loosened the nightmare's grip?

Stick continued to sit in bed thinking, watching the hotel window for signs of daybreak. His thoughts soon drifted from his dream and inner person to a well-preserved collection of Evelyn Laroue images. A precious few of Melvin's images went back as far as childhood. Others were drawn from adolescence. The larger share were taken from the early years of Melvin's adulthood. This latter bunch were framed in deep emotion. More than mere images, they were impressions he had collected with his lips. Yes, he and Evelyn had kissed. Four times, to be exact. Melvin remembered them all. How could he forget when Evelyn's articulate, bright, distinctive spirit was at the core of each experience? Demure yet steady with her affections: as far as Melvin knew, Evelyn wrote the book on womanhood.

The felicitous images quickly faded when Stick heard cattle mooing in the distance. His ranch-hand experience told him the cows were on the move, heading north toward Caldwell. He threw back his sheets and called to Whittle, "Rise up, partner. There's a herd of Texas longhorns coming our way. If we hurry, we can get ahead of them."

"Um. Say what?" Whittle hovered somewhere between sleep and wakefulness. "What's the hurry?"

Stick swung out of bed and grabbed his pants. "The hurry is, we don't want to follow a cattle drive to Wichita — especially when it hasn't rained for three weeks. Get up. I'll fetch our horses from the stable and be right back."

Whittle yawned and rubbed his eyes. "What about breakfast? You said I could buy."

"That will have to wait." Stick pulled on his boots and started for the door. "I'd rather go hungry than eat dust."

◆   ◆   ◆

The Chisholm Trail north of Caldwell was so travel-worn a myopic dimwit could have followed it without getting lost, and to Stick and Whittle, after a week on the unmarked plains, it seemed as if they were journeying upon a crowded highway. Every ten or twenty miles they passed by a homestead, or sheep farm, or met some tradesman heading south. Once they even encountered a stagecoach drawn by four white horses.

Stick and Whittle camped that night alongside the trail. The next day, shortly after noon, they reached the south bank of the Arkansas River, where, after some debate, they boarded a ferry that carried them over to Wichita City. Whittle insisted on paying the fee for the ferry, which was a dollar and forty cents, horses included. He explained to Stick, "It's been a long, long time since I had a new outfit. No sense getting all wet just before making a public appearance."

It had been three years since Stick had been in Wichita City and he was surprised by how much the place had grown. Obviously, like several other cowtowns in Kansas, Wichita City was in the midst of an economic boom. He and Whittle stopped for a few minutes on Douglas Avenue and watched a crew of carpenters at work on a new hotel. Afterwards they proceeded up Second Street, turned left onto Wichita Street, rode ahead to Main Street and stopped again at the Southern Hotel. Stick considered the building for a moment, but after he saw a man standing out front scratching his armpits he decided the establishment did not meet his standards and the duo continued along Main to the Empire Hotel. The Empire was the most luxurious joint in town. It had three floors, two wings and (as Whittle later counted and informed Stick) fifty-two windows.

They rented a top-floor room with two beds for seven dollars a night. It had hooked rugs, brocade curtains, a cushioned couch, a mirror, and fancy, flower-print wallpaper. Whittle was impressed with the room, but thought it was way overpriced and urged Stick to reconsider the Southern, which let rooms for three dollars a night. Stick said no. He suspected the Southern had fleas. The Empire was his treat.

By three that afternoon Stick and Whittle had eaten a late lunch, Ben and Mercy were installed in a stable on the south side of Second Street and Stick was ensconced on the couch in their room, reading a copy of the *Wichita Eagle*. Fresh off the press, the paper was dated Thursday, June 19, 1872.

Spending the afternoon in a hotel room was evidently not Whittle's idea of fun. "For crying out loud," he chaffed at his partner. "We just got here. Don't you want to look around?"

"Maybe later."

"Hmph." The boy shook his head despairingly. "Don't you know reading during the day is a bad habit?"

Stick did not look up or deign to answer.

Whittle huffed and started for the door. "Fine. You stay here. I'm going out. Be back in a little while."

Stick mumbled an absent-minded farewell. His mind was miles away, in Africa where Doctor Livingston had recently arrived in a town called Unyanyembe. The *New York Herald* search commander, Mr. Stanley, had left there with a packet of the Great Explorer's letters and was en route to the coast. While the world waited for Stanley's report, Sir Henry Rawlinson of the Royal Geographical Society in London had formally acknowledged the enterprise of the American press and remarked upon the well-deserved popularity of the *New York Herald*.

The town of Abilene, Kansas, had recently closed its cattle pens and withdrawn from the lucrative but socially disruptive beef-by-rail market. Abilene's ruling powers had fired their trigger-happy sheriff, Wild Bill Hickok, and were looking forward to a more peaceful summer than they'd known in years.

The Santa Fe Railroad was now making regular stops at Dodge City. Construction had begun on a rail line from Wichita City to connect with the Santa Fe, twenty-five miles north of town.

A portion of Drover's Cottage had been dismantled in Abilene and moved to the town of Ellsworth.

On Tuesday a small herd of sixty buffalo had been spotted twenty miles south of Fort Larned.

Stick closed the paper and was about to set it aside when an announcement on the back page caught his eye. A five-thousand-dollar reward offered by Rolland DeJarnette for the safe return of his eleven-year-old daughter and the daughter's governess had been doubled to ten thousand dollars. The two females had been kidnapped on June 13 and were being held for ransom. Anyone interested in helping R. DeJarnette secure the safe return of his daughter and the governess should inquire at Number 12 South Wichita.

Something stirred inside Stick and he reread the announcement. Hmm. Now what had caught his eye? Oh, yes, the name. DeJarnette. It was French-sounding. Could it . . . well, could it be the name the boardinghouse matron in Baltimore had failed to remember?

Calm down, Stick told himself. Don't leap to conclusions.

But something inside wouldn't let him calm down.

What if the announcement *was* referring to Evelyn Laroue? What if *she* was the kidnapped governess?

Kidnapped! Evelyn? How could he not at least investigate? It was the best clue he'd had in eight long years, even if it was a long shot.

Put your boots on. Number 12 South Wichita can't be far, he told himself.

As Stick exited the room and started down the hotel stairs he was struck in the chest by a thought: If Evelyn was indeed the governess kidnapped along with the DeJarnettes' daughter, she'd most likely been living with the family . . . which suggested — just possibly — that she had not married.

Stick soon found a house on South Wichita Street with a plaque on the gate that read: Number 12. For several intensely suspenseful minutes he stood eyeing the brown front door of the white frame house. For him, the door was a fateful threshold: Behind it lay clues to Evelyn Laroue's whereabouts, or crushing disappointment. Perhaps the governess was named Beverly, or Constance, or Jean. He considered running in the opposite direction, but of course he did not. He had to go forward and knock.

An attractive, middle-aged woman wearing a bustled skirt and a high-collared blouse answered the door. She had thick dark hair neatly arranged in a bun on the back of her head and a pair of intelligent brown eyes. Lines under those eyes spoke of many sleepless nights and Stick correctly discerned that this was the mother of the missing girl. "May I help you?" the woman inquired in a beleaguered voice.

The woman's hurt tone stirred up feelings of sympathy within Stick and he felt a pang of guilt. Since reading the announcement he had thought only of Evelyn, and of his own apprehensions, but now, face-to-face with a mother whose child had been stolen, he became aware of a great, all-consuming grief that diminished the relative importance of his own wants and wishes. He removed his sombrero and told the woman, "I have come to speak with Rolland DeJarnette."

"Have you come about the reward?" The woman watched Stick's eyes for clues to his character.

"I read the announcement," Stick answered plainly, pausing a beat before adding, "The reward is not what interests me."

The woman was intrigued. "Oh? What brings you then?"

Stick paused again. The woman deserved an honest answer, yet he was not prepared to reveal his real purpose in presenting himself. Instead, he offered a half-truth. "I cannot abide kidnappers."

The woman seemed to approve of Stick's answer, and of Stick himself. "You strike me as an honest man. Are you brave?"

Stick looked down, not with shame, but out of respect for what bravery was. "I got through the war."

The woman withdrew into the hallway and motioned for Stick to enter the house. "Who shall I say is calling?"

"Melvin Fitchett."

"I'm Florence DeJarnette. Rolland is in the parlor. I'm glad you have come, Mister Fitchett. I pray you can help us."

Stick dipped his head deferentially. There was something admirable and brave about the way Florence DeJarnette wore her sufffering openly and without guise. Somehow, despite her grief, she retained her dignity, and Stick was completely won over to the woman's cause. As he followed her down the dimly lit hallway he sensed that he was already committed to seeing the DeJarnettes reunited with their daughter, even if the girl's governess was not his lost sweetheart.

Rolland DeJarnette was sitting in a tall wingback chair when Florence and Stick entered the parlor. The first thing Stick noticed about the man was his hair, which was silver and neatly arranged in a pompadour. The second thing Stick noticed was that the man's right leg was crippled and shorter than his left leg. Perhaps it had been broken and healed poorly, or maybe stricken by disease. It did not matter. His handicap notwithstanding, the man got up from the chair, glanced pointedly at Stick, then made eye contact with his wife. "Dear," she said to her husband. "This is Mister Fitchett."

Rolland DeJarnette nodded and studied Stick with unveiled interest. Stick studied the man back. There was instant tension. But soon the two men saw something in each other that put them both at ease. From Rolland's perspective: a confident man in his physical prime who had steady eyes. From Stick's perspective: a successful businessman with an admirable wife and a no-nonsense manner about him. For each man, at this stage of the interview, it was all they needed to know about one another. Rolland pointed to a chair opposite his and they both sat down. "Mister Fitchett, are you a professional bounty hunter?"

"No, sir."

Rolland DeJarnette pursed his lips and peered thoughtfully at Stick. After a moment he shrugged and said, "Perhaps that's for the best. So far, all the professional gunslingers in town have refused to get involved with our . . . problem. They're frightened, of course. They don't want anything to do with the man that snatched our daughter. His name is Pascuali Leon. I hear he has a formidable reputation as a killer."

Stick absorbed the information without any visible change of expression.

"Leon is not alone," Rolland DeJarnette continued. "He

has a gang of cutthroats working for him. They took our daughter and her governess six days ago, and are holding them for a ransom of ten thousand dollars. Leon sent one of his minions to the house last week to inform me of his terms. Basically, he promises our daughter and the governess will not be harmed if I pay what he asks, and perhaps that is true. Leon has kidnapped before and returned his hostages in good condition. I suspect he's trying to establish credentials in the kidnapping trade. Damn him. He's a despicable man."

A pause ensued that seemed to need filling, and Stick said, "Kidnappers are the worst."

Rolland DeJarnette agreed, "They're vile animals that can't be trusted. I'd rather give my money to honest men."

"I understand," Stick said softly. And he did understand the spirit of the man's decision, if not the logic of jeopardizing his daughter's safety for the sake of a moral point.

"We want our daughter back, Mister Fitchett. I'd go after her myself if I were fit for rough terrain."

Stick sat forward. "What are the details of Leon's offer?"

"A man is coming here next week, on the twenty-third. Leon wants me to give that man ten thousand dollars cash. If I do, our daughter and the governess will be in Wichita three days later. Leon warns that if his man does not return to him with the money by the twenty-sixth, he will no longer be responsible for the civilized treatment of his hostages. Leon threatens me, Mister Fitchett. The man is scum."

Stick leaned further forward in his chair. "What is your daughter's name?"

The question was answered by Florence DeJarnette, who was standing behind her husband. "Adeline."

Now for the moment of truth. Stick drew a fortifying breath and asked, "And the governess?"

"Miss Laroue," answered Rolland DeJarnette.

"Evelyn," added Florence. "She's been with us since Adeline was three."

Stick said nothing. His body had gone numb from head to toe and it was all he could do to keep hold of the hat in his hand.

Rolland cleared his throat. "To rescue our little girl and Miss Laroue you'll have to go into Leon's lair. Are you prepared to do that, Mister Fitchett?"

Stick managed an affirmative nod.

"Good. I've done some investigating and I'll tell you what I know about Leon's operation. Florence, please get the map from my desk and hand it to the gentleman."

As Stick waited for the map, he wondered if the DeJarnettes could hear his heart pounding in his chest like a war drum.

TWELVE

STICK REMAINED IN the parlor for another hour. During that time he made a copy of the map Rolland DeJarnette had acquired from a retired outlaw named Only Olson. The map purported to show the location of Leon's hideout, yet it was so crudely drawn and lacking in detail that its ultimate value was in doubt. Stick also heard numerous horror stories about Pascuali Leon's criminal past, learned the known facts about Evelyn Laroue and Adeline DeJarnette's abduction and developed a basic plan of action with his host, Adeline's father. In short, Rolland would arrange for Wichita City's sheriff, Fred Schattner, to detain the man that Leon sent to pick up the ransom. This would provide Stick with a few extra days in which to locate the hideout and liberate the hostages. Both men knew it was more of a hopeful scenario than an actual plan, yet they also realized the situation called for bold action. Besides which, their options were limited. Stick agreed wholeheartedly with Rolland DeJarnette when he stated, "The whole enterprise is fraught with danger, but you can't compromise with a man like Leon. I've always believed, you either dance with the devil or you don't."

By the time Stick arose to leave the parlor he had grown to know a little about the DeJarnette family, and by extension, learned something of the peripatetic life Evelyn had been leading since leaving Baltimore. Rolland was a financier in the railroad business and the family had moved dozens of times in the past eight years. In fact, they had only arrived in Wichita City from St. Louis, Missouri, three months before, at which point Rolland had bankrolled the rail line now under construction on the north side of town. Yes, the DeJarnettes were rich folks, but unlike so many other newly affluent frontier families, there was nothing arrogant or presumptuous about them. Stick was relieved to know that Evelyn had been working for such an upstanding couple.

He never told the DeJarnettes that their governess was the calendar, clock and measure of all time in his life. He figured if they were to learn about him and Evelyn, they would do so by sight, or hear it from Evelyn's lips when they returned together to Wichita City with young Adeline in hand.

Florence ushered Stick to the door where she delayed him with a touch. "The man that took Adeline and Evelyn from me must be the evilest person in the world. My husband talked around the matter, Mister Fitchett, but I understand that Leon will try to kill you and the men you take along."

Stick said nothing. If he had misled the DeJarnettes in any way, it was by implying that he would hire a crew of vigilantes to assist him. The truth was, he didn't know anyone in Wichita.

Florence DeJarnette did not care whether Stick was going alone or taking the whole United States Army. Her faith was in him as a man, and she said, "My life has no significance without my daughter. If you must kill Leon to free Adeline and Miss Laroue, please do so in my name and spare yourself the guilt."

Stick peered into the deep wells that were Florence DeJarnette's eyes, letting her know with a look that he understood. Then he placed his sombrero on his head and told Florence, "You rest easy, Ma'am. I'll bring your little girl home."

She followed Stick out the door, watching as he crossed the yard, and called to him when he reached for the gate. "Good luck, Mister Fitchett. May God grant you swift success."

Stick turned, tipped his hat and went. He did not care where he went. He just walked. Had the streets been paved with gold, he never would have noticed. Evelyn Laroue was alive and unmarried. He'd found her . . . or would soon. So what if a gang of mendacious outlaws held her captive in a naturally defensible canyon ninety miles southwest of Wichita: Now that Stick's purpose had been restored in full vigor, he was not going to be stymied by mere logistical challenges. Come monsters or mayhem, he was riding to the rescue in the morning.

Whittle had been scouring the streets of Wichita for more than half an hour when he finally spied his missing partner wandering aimlessly past Schattner's Saloon on the east side of Main Street. Whittle dashed forward and cried angrily. "Stick, where have you been? I was looking all over."

Stick halted and gazed expressionlessly at the boy.

When Whittle saw that Stick's normally sky-blue eyes had turned flat gray he realized something was wrong and went from angry to concerned. "What's the matter? Are you sick?"

Stick opened his mouth to speak, yet no words came out.

"Go ahead," Whittle urged. "I'm on your side."

Stick blinked, slowly emerged from his trance and whispered weakly, "Evelyn has been kidnapped."

"What!?"

Stick made no effort to reply. He had said all there was to say and he was spent.

Whittle noticed out of the corner of his eye that several pedestrians had stopped to gawk at Stick, so he took his partner by the arm and wheeled him around in the direction of the Empire Hotel. "Come on, I better get you to the room. You can tell me everything there."

No other words were uttered until after Stick and Whittle reached the hotel, crossed the lobby and were ascending the stairs. Then Whittle sighed knowingly and remarked, "You're lucky you had a partner searching for you. I knew you were going to need one eventually."

Stick heaved a cryptic sigh and continued climbing the stairs. Even he did not know what he was thinking.

Stick sat on his bed and stared at nothing. Whittle crossed his arms and stood opposite Stick. The boy's whole manner of expression implored his partner to start talking, but much to Whittle's chagrin, Stick did not respond to his visual message. He waited ten seconds, then resorted to a verbal command. "Tell me what happened. What's this about Evelyn being kidnapped?"

Stick held up a hand. "Let me think."

"I'll think with you. Just tell me about what."

"Shush a second."

Whittle glared at Stick with offended disbelief. "Don't tell me to shush. I'll shoot you in the foot."

Stick ignored Whittle and continued thinking.

Whittle gritted his teeth and intensified his glare.

After a moment Stick asked, "When you were exploring, did you come across Delano?"

"No, but I know where it is. I can find it."

Stick nodded and got up from the bed.

Whittle's patience expired and he shouted, "What is going on, Stick? You haven't told me anything yet."

"I will on the way to Delano."

"Why are we going there?"

"I want to see a man named Only Olson." Stick started for the door. "He knows things I need to know."

"About what?"

Stick turned slowly and peered at Whittle with such a grim expression that the boy was frightened — not for himself, but for Stick, who looked as if he'd been mortally wounded. "Only Olson knows the man that kidnapped Evelyn. She and a girl named Adeline DeJarnette are being held for ransom."

"Oh," said Whittle, following Stick out the door. At least now he had a sense of what was going on . . . even if it was a grave sense that boded ill for him and his partner.

They were halfway down the stairs when Stick asked, "Have you got your little gun?"

"It's in my boot. Why?"

"I may need you watching my back tonight."

"Consider it watched," Whittle said succinctly. He had switched into his serious mode.

Delano was a red-light district located about a mile west of Wichita City. There wasn't much to the district other than two dance-hall saloons and a collection of ramshackle huts. Most of the entertainers and service personnel who worked in Delano lived in tents set up behind their respective places of employment. The better-known saloon (or worse known, depending on the moral makeup of the knower) was a raucous joint called Rowdy Joe's. This was where Rolland DeJarnette had told Stick he would be apt to find Only Olson.

On the walk to Delano, Stick told Whittle about spotting the announcement in the paper, going to visit the DeJarnettes and learning of Evelyn Laroue's plight. An array of questions popped into Whittle's mind, yet he suppressed them all. He had promised to watch Stick's back, and — taking that promise to heart — was so busy peering into roadside shadows and throwing furtive glances over his shoulder he didn't have time for a lot of chitchat.

The night was still young when Stick and Whittle strolled through swinging double doors into Rowdy Joe's. Except for a bald-headed bartender polishing glasses, a trio playing cards at a corner table and two brightly attired women at the bar, the place was empty. One of the women was particularly striking. Swirling around her head and shoulders was a festive cloud of butterscotch-colored hair and she wore a sleeveless red dress with a plunging neckline that brazenly emphasized her womanly attributes. To go with all that, she had a bright smile which she flashed at Stick, and then at Whittle. "Howdy, gentlemen." The woman slid off her stool and placed her hands on her shapely hips. "Kate is the name. I'm the matron of the house."

"Hello, Ma'am." Stick removed his sombrero and shyly dipped his head. He could not remember the last time he'd seen so many curves on one person.

"Good evening." Whittle doffed his derby and regarded Kate with an eye for concealed weapons. Thanks to all the parts of her dress that were not there, his investigation was soon complete.

"You fellows are a bit early for the action. The show doesn't start until nine."

"We didn't come for the show. I'm looking for a man that's supposed to be a regular here."

Kate narrowed her eyes suspiciously at Stick. "How do you mean, looking? If you've got a beef to settle with somebody, you better take it elsewhere. We don't cotton to gun fighting here at Rowdy Joe's."

"I'm just looking to talk," Stick said easily. "Do you know Only Olson?"

Kate relaxed and replied, "Sure. He comes in like clockwork at eight-thirty every night. You can't miss him. He's a squat fellow with a square head and he's only got two fingers on each hand."

"Oh," Stick said with a shrug. "I guess we'll wait. Does this place serve dinner?"

"We do." Kate smiled. "It's corned beef and mashed potatoes tonight. Dollar a plate."

"We'll take two." Stick gestured to include Whittle in the order, then moved to sit at a table. "I'll have a whiskey and water with my meal, please. Bring my friend a lemonade."

Kate nodded and was about to turn away when Whittle interjected, "Excuse me. When you said two fingers on each hand, did you mean with thumbs, or without thumbs?"

Kate paused to search her memory before replying, "I believe Only has one thumb, sort of."

"Thank you, Ma'am."

Kate smiled at Whittle, winked at Stick, then turned with a swish of her dress and told the woman sitting at the bar, "Liza, fetch two specials and take them to these gentlemen."

Liza hopped from her stool and hurried to obey.

Rowdy Joe's was beginning to fill with patrons by the time Stick and Whittle finished their meal. A man emerged from a back room, sat down at the piano, cracked his fingers and began to play his highly original version of "Buffalo Gals." The song was evidently a cue, for soon several ladies-of-the-night appeared at the top of an open stairway and sashayed down into the saloon. One of the ladies made a beeline for Stick, but he frowned and shooed her away before she could get any notions. She frowned and said with a look that Stick didn't know what he was missing.

Of course, Stick did know what he was missing, or rather, who . . . and it irritated him to be sitting idly in Rowdy Joe's while Evelyn Laroue was in imminent need of his help. Indeed, he would have been gone from Wichita if not for the need to speak with Only Olson. Without Only's help, Stick knew his chances of finding Leon's lair were slim to none. So he waited . . . and with him waited his body-guard, Whittle, who sat back in his chair, roaming the room with his eyes, missing nothing.

THIRTEEN

AT HALF PAST eight a shorter-than-normal, barrel-chested man with a combined total of four fingers and one stubby thumb ambled into the saloon. Stick stood and caught the man's eye. "If you're Only Olson, I'd like to buy you a whiskey."

The man shot a puzzled look at Stick, glanced at Whittle and returned his attention to Stick. "I don't recollect the pleasure of us meeting before."

"We haven't," said Stick, who sat and added, "which is why I'd like to buy you a whiskey."

Only Olson wriggled his nose disdainfully. "Maybe I ain't in the mood for drinking with strangers."

Stick kicked an empty chair from the table and said in a commanding tone, "Sit down, Only. I got your name from Rolland DeJarnette. We need to talk."

In a flash, Only's gruff demeanor dissolved and his attitude toward Stick changed completely. He sat, leaned across the table and said in a hushed voice, "There's too many ears in Rowdy Joe's. We'll have to go elsewhere to talk. First, though, I'll have that whiskey. Better make it a double."

Ten minutes later, after Only quaffed his drink in a

single gulp and Stick paid the bill for the table, Whittle and the two men arose to depart. Out on the street, Only signalled for Stick and Whittle to follow, and then, without a word of explanation, started walking east toward Wichita City. It seemed to Stick that Only was being overly cautious about matters . . . but then it occurred to him that Only had once ridden with Leon and was in a better position than he to understand the threat the man imposed. One thing was clear: Only was terrified of Pascuali Leon.

Only did not speak until the threesome were climbing a set of outdoor stairs to his rented room above Billy Thompson's Barber Shop on North Main Street. "We can talk freely up here. It's plenty private."

The room was sparsely furnished with a cot, a table, an oil lamp, two chairs and a dresser. Only fished a box of matches from his shirt pocket and deftly lit the oil lamp with the two fingers on his right hand. Stick sat in one of the chairs, Only sat in the other and Whittle stood with arms crossed, leaning against the door. "Now let me get this straight," Only began. "You claim that Rolland DeJarnette sent you to find me."

"No." Stick shook his head. "Rolland showed me the map you drew to Leon's hideout. I asked where I might find you. It was my idea."

"Okay. So you found me."

"I'd like to hire you to guide me to that canyon."

"That's what I was afraid of."

"Afraid?" Stick inquired.

Only snorted derisively. "I'm no coward, Stick, or whatever your real name is. I'm afraid for fools like you that think they can go up against Pascuali Leon. If you had any sense, you'd be heading in the opposite direction."

Whittle would not tolerate such rude treatment of his partner and he angrily interjected, "Hold it, Mister. You don't know Stick or you wouldn't have said that. He's got more sense than you'll ever have."

Only threw an amused glance at the boy, then said dryly to Stick, "My apologies if I offended you. It was just my way of saying that Leon is a shrewd devil. He likes to skin his enemies and eat them for breakfast."

Stick was not deterred. "I just need you to lead me to the canyon, Only. You don't have to get involved."

"I won't," Only replied with alacrity. "And if you take my advice, neither will you. I told Rolland DeJarnette to pay the ransom and thank Leon for not asking more."

"And I told him I would bring his daughter home," Stick countered calmly. "The decision is made. I'm going after the girl and the governess . . . with or without your help."

Only studied Stick closely before asking, "Why? To get your head shot off for ten thousand dollars?"

"I don't care about the money."

"You don't?" Only chortled. "Pray tell, are you crazy?"

Stick stiffened and informed Only in an icy tone. "No. I'm not crazy. I'm duty bound."

"What? You kin to the DeJarnettes or something?"

Stick hesitated a moment, then lied, "The fact is . . . the governess they took, she's my sister."

"Oh." Only sat back and considered Stick anew. Eventually, he sighed and held up his mangled hands for Stick to view. "If you're duty bound, I reckon there's nothing I can say to stop you. But take a good look at what Leon did to me before you go rushing into his snake pit. He sawed off my trigger fingers with a rusty knife, all on account of I said something rude to his woman." Only lowered his hands and continued, "Anyhow, don't get me wrong about Leon. I'd love to cut out his guts and feed them to a buzzard."

"Then come," Stick said hopefully. "Show me the way."

"Nope." Only was adamant. "It ain't much, but I've got me a life here in Wichita. I aim to keep it."

Stick sighed forlornly. "If you won't come, will you at least take a look at my maps and show me what I need to know?"

"Sure, but even if you find the canyon, you won't be rescuing anybody out of there."

"What makes you so certain?"

"The canyon," Only replied simply, then explained, "I was with Leon the day some Cheyennes chased us in there. We wouldn't have found it if we weren't running desperate. Anyhow, the canyon is closed in by rocky walls and surrounded by open prairie on three sides. It's got a good spring right in the middle of it, and a couple of log huts, so they can sit in there as long as they have food. Plus, there's a high butte at the point of the canyon with a perfect lookout station, so you can't reach it without being watched, and when you get there, you can't get in without a personal invitation. The entrance is so narrow, horses have to ride single file."

Stick reached into his shirt and withdrew the two maps: his original, plus the one he had drawn in the DeJarnettes' parlor. He lay the maps on the table and muttered with conviction, "I'll get in there, one way or the other."

"It's your funeral," Only allowed, leaning forward to study Stick's handiwork. "I reckon if you can find Bear Creek, you'll stand a fair chance of finding the canyon."

Whittle's curiosity was piqued and he moved from the doorway toward the table. Stick had not told him about the second map, nor had he said anything about a reward. These matters were of some interest to Whittle, yet what really grabbed his attention was Only's mention of Bear Creek. That was where Brings the Rain had said she and Talking Rock were headed.

After eyeing the maps a moment, Only took a pencil and an eraser from a table drawer, clasped the pencil with the fingers on his right hand and palmed the eraser with his shortened thumb. Then — with surprising dexterity and a modicum of artistic merit — he made several minor modifications to the map. He explained as he worked, "There's another creek after the Medicine Lodge. I don't know what it's called, but it's not the one you're looking for. If you stay south you'll hit the Nescutunga. That's due west of Bear Creek by maybe a dozen miles or more. Bear Creek has two forks. They meet somewhere about . . . here." Only marked the spot with an X, made eye contact with Stick, then added a series of scratches around the mark. "There's a bit of woods around Bear Creek, mostly evergreens, and about five miles north of where the forest ends you'll come to half a dozen small hills, one right after the other. Beyond the last hill stands a solitary sandstone butte. The butte overlooks the canyon entrance." Only drew another X and sat back. "Whichever way you go, you'll have to cross open land."

"Maybe at night," Stick proposed.

Only grunted. He didn't care to speculate.

Stick folded his maps, returned them to his shirt and stood. "Thanks for your help, Only."

"You might not be thanking me once Leon and his gang

get a bead on you. He'll have at least five men with him. Not a one of them has ever been to church."

Stick hesitated before starting toward the door. Although he was fearful of the answer, there was one more question he had to ask. "Leon told DeJarnette the hostages wouldn't be harmed. My sister is a good-looking woman. What are the chances of the men letting her be?"

Only perceived Stick's concern and seemed genuinely pleased to offer an encouraging reply. "The chances are better than you might think, thanks to Leon's witch, Sadie Culpepper. Pascuali knows she'd slit his throat if he touched another woman and he's far too cruel to let his men enjoy a pleasure he can't have. Don't worry about your sister, at least not until after the payoff date. She should be safe until then."

Stick was visibly relieved. "Thanks again, Only. You're a good man."

Only snickered. "Never been accused of that before."

Stick and Whittle were on Main Street, walking toward the Empire Hotel, when Whittle wondered, "So, Stick, why'd you tell Only that Evelyn was your sister?"

"Easier than trying to explain."

"Oh," said Whittle, content to let the matter lie.

They walked a ways further and then, to Whittle's

surprise, Stick elaborated of his own accord, "The truth is, I haven't seen Evelyn in more than eight years. It wouldn't be right for me to call her my sweetheart. Besides, Evelyn was always high-spirited. For all I know, she may have forgotten who I am and turned sweet on some other man."

Whittle sounded an incredulous note. "I don't believe that. And neither do you."

"No," Stick said softly, "not in my heart. But the world is a peculiar place, Whittle. It would be foolish of me not to admit the possibility of some change."

"The world is peculiar," Whittle agreed. "That much I know. And I also know that you worry too much, Stick."

"Well, right now I've got a lot on my mind."

"Of course you do, which is why you ought not to worry. The brain is only so big. You'll just wear yourself out."

Stick cocked an eye at Whittle and said, "You've got a point there. It's a unique one, but it's a point."

Stick and Whittle had been in their hotel room for nearly five minutes without a word passing between them. Stick was sitting on the foot of one bed and Whittle was across from him, on the foot of the other bed. The boy was patiently waiting for a reply to the question he had asked. Finally Stick answered, "I'm not sure we are going to do anything."

Whittle's eyes darkened. "What do you mean by that?"

"I mean we've had a pretty good run together," Stick said in a firm yet gentle tone. "Perhaps we'll have another go at it in the future, but in the morning we'll be parting ways."

"Hogwash."

"Whittle . . . you don't want to go where I'm going. There's a strong chance I won't be coming back."

The boy became hotly indignant. "What do you think I am, a fair-weather friend? Please, don't insult me."

"I'm just telling you how it's going to be."

Whittle huffed. "There you go again, appointing yourself head of this outfit. Forget about us parting ways. You're not going to face those outlaws alone."

"I don't think you understand," Stick tried to reason with the lad. "This isn't a game you can quit when things get ugly. And they will get ugly. It's best I go without you."

"No," Whittle fired back. "You don't understand. This is my chance to do good for the world. Remember, I told you that was my purpose. Like you said, it's everyone's manifest destiny to go where they want and do good. So you better accept it. Besides, after we rescue the girls, you'll need help getting them back to Wichita. And on top of that, even if we did part ways — which we aren't — I'd just be on my way to Bear Creek. Without you, I might as well go looking for Brings the Rain."

Stick frowned as hard as he could frown.

Whittle laughed.

"What?" Stick asked with intense annoyance.

Whittle struggled to stop laughing. "To be completely honest with you, Stick, I can hardly wait to see what Evelyn does when she learns you aren't dead."

"Unless I wind up dead," Stick snapped. "That's what I'm trying to tell you. Dead may be what happens."

"Dead don't scare me."

"It does when you see it close."

"I've seen dead close. I helped bury Slender Thomas. Dug most of the grave myself. I won't try to say I'm fond of dead, but it doesn't scare me."

Stick paused. Some things in life, he knew, were inevitable, and this seemed to be one of them. Also, in the back of his mind he realized he would probably wish for assistance on several occasions in the coming days. Finally he relented. "You'll have to do exactly what I say. No arguments about who made me the boss. If I say sit ten miles away, you'll sit. Understand?"

"Yep."

"All right then. Presuming we don't wind up dead and we get the job done, we'll split the reward fifty-fifty."

"Thanks, partner. Five grand will do me right. Now, quit talking dead. That's worse than reading in the daytime."

FOURTEEN

IT TOOK NEARLY two hours for Stick and Whittle
to accomplish everything they wanted to do before leaving
Wichita City the next morning. By the time they mounted
up and started out of town the clock had already struck
nine.

Stick rode in front on Mercy, who was no longer encumbered by the full weight of her master's personal belongings.
Except for his Sharps long gun, bedroll, telescope and saddlebag stuffed with incidentals, Stick's gear was stored in a
locker at the Empire Hotel. Whittle followed on Ben,
whose lips were purple after eating the contents of a can of
plums for breakfast. Behind Ben and Whittle was a gray,
swayback mare purchased an hour earlier for fifty dollars.
That was twice her fair value, yet she was pliable and had
been available for a quick sale, and Stick had been in no
mood to haggle over money. Whittle took an immediate
liking to the old horse and named her Miss Prescott. She
now carried blankets (bought for the hostages), a coil of
rope, two pounds of beef jerky, a bag of oats and ten boxes
of ammunition. Two boxes were for Stick's Sharps Fifty
Caliber; the other eight were for the matching cock-action

Winchester rifles Stick had obtained for sixty dollars apiece.

In most towns around the world, at most times of day, people would halt and take notice of two fellows riding past with rifles slung over their shoulders, yet this was not so on the Kansas frontier in 1872. In fact, on this Friday in June as the duo set forth no one so much as batted an eye.

Stick was glad for anonymity. From the way Only Olson had behaved at the mere mention of Pascuali Leon's name, Stick figured the fewer people aware of his existence the better. He was operating under the assumption that surprise would be his most effective weapon in his assault upon the canyon. He could only hope that Leon and his gang felt so secure in their hideout their defensive vigilance had grown lax.

Nary a soul was stirring in Delano when Stick and Whittle rode through. (Nights were long in the entertainment business and few folks in the district ever awoke before noon.) The prairie waited a short distance beyond the entrance to Rowdy Joe's. Here in the wide open, Whittle felt free to converse with Stick. Indeed, the boy was compelled to speak. His partner was tenser than a tightly-drawn bow and clearly needed to be distracted. Whittle rode up beside Stick and casually ventured, "Dry out here, isn't it?"

"Yep."

"Just wondering, why all the rope?"

"Had a hunch it might come in handy."

"I see." Whittle paused, then wondered, "Are you pale, or is it my imagination? Did you have that dream again?"

"No," Stick said sourly, adding with a weary sigh, "I was awake all night thinking. I didn't dream a thing."

"Oh. So are you going to be grouchy all day?"

"I might."

"You know, Stick, just because all the odds are stacked against us, it doesn't mean we have to have miserable attitudes."

"Whittle . . ."

"What?"

"Shush. I'm trying to concentrate."

"Pardon me," Whittle replied in a bruised tone. "I was just trying to help you relax."

"I appreciate the sentiment, but right now I need to think. Surely you can understand that."

"Yeah, I understand," Whittle replied glumly. He let Ben fall in line behind Mercy and gave Miss Prescott plenty of slack. Whittle had wanted to ask if he could shoot some practice rounds with his new rifle, but he realized now wasn't a good time to inquire about anything and decided to broach the matter later.

Meanwhile Stick was thinking: Better keep to the south and avoid the possibility of encountering Leon's emissary on his way to Wichita. It's a long shot, but it could happen. We'll swing around and hit Bear Creek above the Kansas border, then work our way northwest from there. Now let's see. Today is the twentieth. The ransom is due on the twenty-third. Figure three days' travel to the canyon. Leon will be expecting his pickup man to return on the twenty-sixth. That gives me six days . . . maybe a week before trouble starts. Agh. It's been a long time since I shot anyone. Oh well. Guns attract guns and kidnappers are vermin. It's not like I'll be aiming at innocent citizens. I probably should have bought some dynamite. What am I going to do with the boy? Can't let him get killed. The tenacious rascal — he got those plums he wanted. He was right, too. It is dry. Hmm. With luck we'll hit the Ne-ne-scah River by noon. Maybe make the Shawacospah by dark. I was foolish, paying so much for that old nag. Good rifles though. Worth every penny. Ooo . . . Sweet Evelyn. You hold on. I'm coming. Those sorry criminals better not touch a hair on your head. Melvin Fitchett will teach them some manners.

Stick soon emerged from his ruminations and called over his shoulder to Whittle, "Come on, let's pick up the pace and see what Miss Prescott is made of."

"Pick it up all you want," Whittle replied, "and don't

worry about Miss Prescott. She may be ugly as a pig's rear end, but she's too polite to fall behind."

"Good. I like a well-mannered nag."

They crossed the Ne-ne-scah River an hour or so after noon, paused long enough to let the horses drink, then pushed on at a hard trot. Two hours later they came to a small creek with a grove of sandbar willows shading the foot of a knoll on the south bank. Whittle dismounted and wondered, "What's this called?"

Stick studied the map that Only Olson had modified. After a moment he said with a shrug, "Don't know. It's not marked."

"At least it's not a river," Whittle noted. "The way they name streams out here on the plains, it's enough to give English a bad reputation. I mean, if that Ne-ne-whatever-you-said is a river, what do you call the Mississippi?"

For the first time on this day, the slim makings of a smile appeared on Stick's face. "I'd call it a big river."

Although Whittle didn't think Stick's quip was particularly funny, he was pleased to observe that his partner's sense of humor had not abandoned him altogether. And noting that, Whittle decided to address the matter he had been suppressing since morning. "So, Stick, I've never shot a rifle before. How about giving me a lesson?"

Stick considered the setting with a sweeping gaze, let his eyes come to rest on Whittle, and after pausing reflectively, allowed, "That may be a good idea."

"I have those on occasion," Whittle retorted dryly.

They stood with the creek behind them and faced the north slope of the knoll. Stick showed the boy how to load and cock the Winchester into firing position. He warned him against traveling with bullets in the chamber, took the cardboard top off one of the ammunition boxes, walked to the base of the knoll, placed the top on its side, then returned to Whittle and instructed, "Aim for a second or two and listen to the rhythm of your heart. You want to time your shot between heartbeats. When you're ready, draw gently on the trigger. Don't pull. Imagine you're squeezing a bag of dead mice."

Whittle eyed Stick dubiously. "Dead mice?"

Stick explained, "It's a way of saying squeeze the trigger gently. Winchester rifles are sensitive."

"Okay. Where do you want me to hit the target?"

Stick snorted. "Shoot for the center. You'll likely miss the whole thing. Now go ahead. Let's see how close you come."

Whittle steadied the rifle stock against his shoulder, counted the beats of his heart . . . one . . . two, then drew back on the trigger. *Bap.*

Stick took two steps toward the target, squinted, then whirled to face Whittle and declared, "There's beginner's luck for you. You hit it square in the middle." Stick retreated from the boy's field of vision and instructed, "Take another shot. Let's see what happens."

Whittle cocked a bullet into the firing chamber, counted his heartbeats and squeezed. *Bap.* He cocked again quickly and fired again. *Bap.*

Stick strode forward and peered at the target for several seconds. Both shots had kissed the previous bull's-eye. He turned doubtfully to Whittle and inquired, "You sure you've never shot a rifle before?"

"Not that I remember," Whittle answered honestly. "And I'm not that old. I wouldn't have forgot."

Stick glanced at the target, looked at Whittle, removed his sombrero and offered, "Never seen anything like it. You're a natural."

A proud grin flashed over Whittle's face. "I always figured a rifle would be more accurate than a derringer." He hoisted the gun to his shoulder. "Watch. One more."

Bap.

Stick went slack-jawed. The shot was wide of dead center by the thickness of a thumbnail. In a flash, he realized he'd been wrong about Whittle. The boy was not a liability. The boy was an asset. At the very least,

Stick was glad to know Whittle would not be shooting at him.

Night found them still looking for the Shawacospah River. They tethered the horses, chewed on beef jerky for supper and lay down under the stars. (Even if there had been wood for a fire, Stick would not have lit one and risked smoke-signalling their presence on the plains. With such precaution in mind, he'd left his cooking utensils in Wichita and planned to go without his customary morning cup of coffee.) They'd been on their backs for about fifteen minutes when a burgeoning moon appeared on the horizon and bathed the world around them in a soft, silvery light. The moon was two nights shy of full.

Stick ended a silent spell, saying, "You know, Whittle, you don't have to keep with me. It was brave of you to come this far, but you can go off when we hit Bear Creek, if you want."

"Trying to ditch me again?"

"No. Reminding you of your independence."

"That's gentlemanly of you, but I don't need reminding. Fact is, I've been making my own decisions all along."

Stick smiled and said nothing. It was true. Whittle consistently marched to his own drum. Indeed, the boy did so now, saying, "Stick, I've been meaning to ask, do you believe in God?"

Stick mused a moment before replying, "I'm God-fearing, if that's what you're asking. Do you believe?"

"You bet," Whittle said with alacrity. "Who else could make the stars? But I asked you first. Does fearing mean believing?"

Stick sighed heavily. "It does in the heart."

"That's a roundabout answer."

"Simply put, yes, I believe in God, although for me there's more to it. If you want, I'll tell you something I learned at Wilderness."

"Sure I want."

Stick spoke slowly and evenly. "The day before the battle at Wilderness everyone knew a wicked fight was coming. Grant wanted to crush us and run to Richmond. And Lee was anxious to right some mistakes that were made at Gettysburg. All that day while we were waiting for the Union Army to find us, a lot of men got the feeling they were going to die. It was a strong feeling — more than fear — it was almost a kind of knowledge that settled over the field. Anyhow, Lee was a religious man and everybody looked up to him, and because of who he was, thousands of soldiers suddenly decided to get right with God before the fight started and there was a rush to visit the chaplain. Poor old man. He was overwhelmed affirming people's commitment to God. He was blessing groups of a hundred or more at a time."

"And you?" Whittle wondered. "Did you get blessed?"

"No. But not because I don't believe, or didn't then. It was more a matter of not wanting to decide something because I was afraid of dying. Also . . . well, it struck me that a lot of men were trying to bargain with God, and I don't believe that's proper. Now, it's not my place to judge . . . yet one thing I noticed after the fight was that lots of men that got the chaplain's blessings were dead, and lots of them that didn't affirm, lived. Of course, it went both ways in large numbers — so that doesn't prove a thing — which I'm not trying to do anyway. I'm only saying I get confused trying to comprehend God. For me, Whittle, it makes more sense to believe in simple ideas."

"Simple like what?"

"Well, like luck. I can grasp that."

Whittle took a moment to digest Stick's words. Then he volunteered, "I admit, when I see a sick baby, or a hungry dog, or a dead bird or something, it makes me wonder what God is up to. As for luck, I've never had much of that."

"I don't know. You came this far."

Whittle looked around and gestured at the moonlit prairie. "You call this lucky?"

Stick chuckled. "No, maybe not. Still, a youngster growing up on his own, I suspect you've had more luck than you realize."

Whittle shrugged. "I reckon."

Stick yawned and clasped his hands behind his head. "Let's get some sleep. We've got a long bunch of days ahead."

"You mean years, don't you?" Whittle corrected his partner. "We've got a long bunch of years ahead of us. Not days."

"If you say so. I hope you're right."

Whittle grinned at the moon and quipped, "I usually am right. Haven't you noticed? And by the way, don't let those bandits worry you. I predict you and Evelyn will get married one day and have a whole passel of kids."

"Whittle."

"What?"

"Shush."

"Yes, boss." The boy rolled over on his blanket. "My lips are sealed. I won't say another word until tomorrow morning, except good night. I forgot to tell you that."

Stick groaned.

"Ssh," whispered Whittle.

FIFTEEN

MELVIN FITCHETT WAS dreaming. In his dream he was Stick and he was dreaming of Melvin's experience at Wilderness. Yet the dream was different. It had changed and did not haunt him as before. It continued to change as he dreamed.

Soldiers were in the pine forest. Bullets were whizzing by in the growing dark. Melvin cried triumphantly to every passing slug, "Ha. You missed me." Ezekiel Beck approached. He held a yellowing tintype in his hand. He told Melvin, "My sister could make Jeb Stuart blush." Melvin smelled smoke and looked up. The tip of a pine tree burst into flames, and in an instant the fire spread to surrounding trees. Ezekiel dropped the tintype and pointed. "Look. There's Lee." Melvin turned and saw Robert E. Lee walking through the raging inferno. The general nodded to Melvin and said, "Even the devil is scared of rolling fire." Suddenly, the great man dissolved in a puff of smoke. Ezekiel advised, "Let him go." Then Melvin's vision was obscured by a curtain of red. He found himself on a hospital cot watching a spider crawl across the ceiling. Robert E. Lee whispered in Melvin's ear, "Remember the rolling fire."

Stick awoke and sat up in the predawn light. Mercy saw him stir and whinnied softly. Stick greeted her with a click of his tongue, then began to analyze his changed dream. Mostly, he asked questions. What did the new dream mean? And why had it changed now, after eight years of sameness? Had he changed? Did Evelyn's nearby presence influence the shape of his dream? Was there a person inside of him trying to speak? Or was that a case of Slender Thomas expounding myths for an impressionable boy?

Agh. Stick sensed that he was grabbing at straws. A dream was just a dream. It could mean anything. Or nothing. Still, something had shifted — be it inside or out of Stick, he did not know — and the world seemed somehow looser now and more filled with possibilities.

Cease this woolgathering, Stick berated himself mentally. The dream changed. So what, it's only a dream. You've got a canyon to find.

He lifted his gaze to the sky where a bank of swift-moving cirrocumulus clouds ushered in the dawn. Gray with moisture, the clouds rushed down from the north. Stick stiffened as the ominous formations approached. He'd worked long enough on open ranges in Texas to know when unsettled weather was approaching. Everything he saw told him to rise and get moving.

They crossed the Medicine Lodge River at mid-morning. It wasn't deep or particularly wide, but it ran harmoniously through the landscape and Whittle had no qualms about calling it a river. Near noon they reached a diminutive branch of the Nescutunga. Stick followed the feeder stream south toward the main course of the river. He had no intentions of turning westward until he was well beyond the Nescutunga.

As they continued along, a layer of nimbostratus clouds drifted up from the south and began to slide under the higher-altitude cirrocumulus clouds. It was not a good sign. The two systems flowed in contrary directions, rolling and churning the air between them with growing intensity. Clearly, trouble was brewing overhead.

Oh, hell, Stick reflected. *Trouble is everywhere this week. What's a little atmospheric agitation next to Pascuali Leon and his lawless minions?*

The duo did not hear the first rumble of thunder until late in the afternoon. They had just crossed the Nescutunga and were riding ashore on the south bank when the sky began to grumble. The timing seemed more than coincidental to Whittle, who noted, "There appears to be a dividing line here."

"Does, doesn't it," Stick agreed.

They gained dry ground and halted. Immediately thereafter another rumble of thunder reverberated around them. Whatever the sky was trying to say, it was serious.

"What do you think?" Whittle wondered. His question was punctuated by a loud crackle of lightning.

"I think we're in for a storm and that things are going to get a lot worse before they get better."

"True," Whittle concurred with a nod, adding, "but worse for the kidnappers. Not us. I feel that in my bones. We're going to be fine."

"You've got the right attitude. Now come on," said Stick, riding forth on Mercy. "We want to find Bear Creek before dark."

"We will, even if it takes flying," Whittle chirped as he nudged Ben's flanks and followed his partner's lead. Little did the boy imagine the prophetic power of his own words.

It seemed to Stick like a long dozen miles from where the travelers crossed the Nescutunga to where Only Olson said they would find Bear Creek, and the further he and Whittle journeyed without any sign of an evergreen forest, the more Stick began to question whether Only had purposefully misled them. All the while lightning flashed over the plains with increased frequency and the wind whooshed and whirred around them. It was not long before it began to rain. They rode on. There was no shelter to seek.

Finally, Stick saw a blurred line of green rising in the distance. He turned, and before shooting off at a gallop, called through the wind and rain to Whittle. "I see the Bear Creek forest. Let's hurry. We'll rest the horses there."

"Go," Whittle replied with a holler. He held his derby and Miss Prescott's lead with his left hand, and in his right he held Ben's reins, which he flicked at the pony's neck. Ben shot forward, yet just as he did a voluminous crackle of lightning rent the air above the party and spooked Miss Prescott. She turned and bolted eastward. The maneuver caught Whittle unaware, yanking him backwards and toppling him from his mount. By some weird turn of luck, the boy landed on his feet, yet in the same moment a forceful gale grabbed his derby and whisked it across the prairie in the opposite direction from Miss Prescott. In the next instant the boy was startled by the sound of a train roaring toward him. What?! He turned toward the sound. It wasn't a train. It was a twister with a hundred-foot-wide funnel!! Suddenly the wind velocity tripled and the roaring became a scream.

In the subsequent seven seconds Whittle was roughly aware of five events. (1) Stick and Mercy had stopped in the distance and Stick was gesticulating wildly at the sky. (2) A wool blanket sailed past Whittle's head. (3) Ben sprinted toward Mercy and Stick. (4) Whittle ran after Ben. (5) A claw reached out from the funnel cloud and plucked Whittle off the ground.

After the fifth event the boy wasn't aware of much, or rather, he was aware of so much he couldn't comprehend his own thoughts. Before he realized what had happened he was more than a hundred feet above terra firma.

Stick watched in horror as Whittle zoomed over the plains with all the instability of a dry leaf on a blustery autumn day. Then the twister took an abrupt turn west toward Stick, Mercy and Ben. Neither man nor horse nor pony hesitated. Collectively they turned and raced for the forest. As hard as Stick was riding and concerned as he was for his own life, his soul had already begun to ache. *Poof.* Just like that: Melvin Smyte had been snatched from earth . . . lofted into the heavens . . . and gone to keep company with his old friend, Slender Thomas. Stick thought he might cry. Partners of Whittle's caliber came along once in a lifetime — and then only if one was lucky. And to some degree, Stick was lucky, for the screaming twister soon turned again and swooped south of him and the panicked horses.

Whittle was confused. The monster had gone away. The world was quiet. He wasn't flying anymore. He was on his back. Above him the evening sky was painted in soft pastels. A beautiful sunset was in progress.

Whittle presumed he was alive . . . yet he wasn't sure. He counted his fingers. Eight, plus two thumbs made ten. He felt his teeth with his tongue. All there. So where was he?

He had to coach himself into moving. Turn your head and look. You'll see something. Now one-and-a-two-and-a-three. Go. When Whittle rolled his head to the left he tipped the delicate balance that held him on the lip of land where the twister had set him down. Having upset that balance, gravity assumed control and he plummeted downward for approximately thirty inches. Bear Creek welcomed him with a splash.

It is beyond the capacity of words to describe what Whittle was thinking and feeling when he hit the water. Let us just say he was flummoxed. Even so, he managed to find the solid bottom of the creek and stand on his feet. He'd hardly accomplished this when a voice cried, "Whee-tal?"

Whittle was not sure of his own mental state. After all, in the previous two hundred and twenty-nine seconds he'd fallen from his pony and lost his derby, been violently yanked into heaven and blown about like a piece of dust, then magically released from the mayhem, set gently upon his back and dropped blindly into a creek. Nevertheless, he was pretty certain that someone had called his name. Or sort of his name.

"Whee-tal?"

There it was again.

The boy turned. It was Brings the Rain, holding a rifle she had scooped from the ground seconds before. She had an astonished look on her face. So did he. They were both temporarily at a loss for words. Eventually Whittle recovered and — determined to get at least one thing straight in the world — informed Brings the Rain, "The name is Whittle."

The girl whispered a few words in the Cheyenne language, then said softly, "Whee-tal."

"Wi. Wi," said Whittle. "Not we, we."

"Whittle."

"That's better. Hello, Brings the Rain. How are you?"

Brings the Rain did not move or speak. When Whittle started toward the creek bank, she gestured for him to halt and asked, "You came on the wind?"

Whittle shrugged. It seemed a reasonable explanation to him.

Brings the Rain's eyes went wide with awe. "Are you with the Wind-being?"

Whittle shook his head. "No. I'm with Stick. At least I was. Don't you remember, we ate pickled eggs together."

Brings the Rain paused dubiously before answering, "Yes, I remember. But you have new clothes."

"Got 'em in Caldwell. Stick gave them to me. Now relax, I'm coming ashore. I won't hurt you."

Brings the Rain was mesmerized by Whittle, who stood before her with his little fingers in his ears, swishing out the water. Suddenly the mysterious traveler's face twitched, then his legs wobbled, his arms trembled, his hands tingled and he sank to the ground in shock.

After the tornado left the area, Stick tethered Ben to a cedar tree and rode Mercy back onto the plains. Despite a fearful apprehension about what he might find, he headed for the spot where he'd last seen Whittle. Although the logic of what he'd seen told Stick the boy was dead, a deep affection for his partner compelled him to search for . . . well, for whatever was out there to be found.

Stick came upon Miss Prescott some five hundred yards east of the forest. He might not have recognized the old girl if not for the length of rope snarled around her crumpled, dead body. He dismounted and began the unpleasant task of disentangling the rope, which he might yet need. While performing this chore he found a bag of oats and two cartons of ammunition. The cartons were as good as new and each held bullets for the Winchester rifles. Looking at the cartons, Stick was poignantly reminded of Whittle's natural sharpshooting skills. He winced and bit his bottom lip. Be it by the will of God or a turn of luck, he could feel the universe pressuring him in and out. Stick knew he was going to miss Whittle for all his remaining hours, days, weeks, months or years on earth.

He secured the rope, rode over the plains in ever-widening circles and found nary a trace of the boy.

Finally, as the colorful sunset dimmed to gray and dusk submitted to darkness, Stick turned Mercy westward and started back toward the forest.

Mercy saw the bowler hat before Stick and veered toward it without waiting for his command. She trotted to the derby, halted over it, sniffed the air, then raised her head and neighed plaintively. Stick dropped to the ground, picked up the hat and began to cry as he had not cried since long before the war and Evelyn Laroue's disappearance. He was mightily sad.

SIXTEEN

A PUNGENT AROMA overwhelmed Whittle and he
awoke from his slumber. Someone had brought a stick of
burning sage into the brushwood hut where he was lying.
The boy sneezed and opened his eyes. He was barefoot. His
new boots and socks had been removed. He sensed a nearby
presence and lifted his head to look. There was just enough
moonlight in the wickiup for him to discern the distinctive
features of Brings the Rain's grandfather, Talking Rock. At
first Whittle was delighted . . . then he thought: Maybe
we're both dead.

But Whittle did not feel dead — not with the smoke
burning his eyes and stimulating his olfactory receptors. He
sneezed again and sat up. Talking Rock reached over to
touch his hand, said something in Cheyenne and crawled
from the hut through a hide-covered exit. Whittle understood that he should follow and did. The first thing he saw
as he emerged from the wickiup were his boots and socks,
laid out to dry. Then he saw Brings the Rain. She sat by
Bear Creek on a bed of moss in a shimmering pool of moonlight. Her long hair was loosened from its braids and she

smiled when she saw Whittle. He almost fainted all over again.

Whittle walked forward and stared with unabashed joy at Brings the Rain, who in his eyes embodied the most perfect beauty the world had to offer. As far as he was concerned, a crown of radiant jewels would not have enhanced her loveliness one iota. She lowered her eyes and blushed shyly under the indiscreet thrust of his gaze. He didn't care if his feelings were apparent; he couldn't have hidden them if he tried.

It required great personal control for Whittle to withdraw his eyes from Brings the Rain when Talking Rock approached from a nearby fire pit and handed him a strip of venison. The boy turned slowly, accepted the meat and nodded appreciatively. Talking Rock grunted with amusement and walked away. Whittle wondered if he could see the hand of fate weaving filaments of moonlight around him and Brings the Rain and did not wish to get caught in the tapestry.

After Whittle ate, he and Brings the Rain found their voices. She wanted to know how Whittle had come to be in her corner of the world. He told her about Stick and Evelyn, about the DeJarnettes, about coming after the kidnappers in the canyon, and about how the twister had plucked him off the plains, tossed him hither and thither, then set his body by the creek where she had found him. Whittle, in his turn, wanted to know about Talking Rock and whether he'd sung his Death-song, and what sort of plans did Brings the Rain have for the future? She told him how her grandfather was enjoying his childhood lands and waiting for a sign before he began to sing. As for her future plans, she too was waiting for a sign.

Whittle grinned knowingly and asked, "By sign, do you mean like someone falling from the sky?"

Brings the Rain pretended to consider and feigned ambiguity. She was having as much fun as Whittle.

They talked awhile of small matters such as plums, pickled eggs, and creeks called rivers, then found themselves running out of words. Eventually they fell silent, content just to observe each other in the moonlight. Later, when Talking Rock brought more venison for Whittle, Brings the Rain told her grandfather about Stick and the gang of kidnappers in the canyon. The old man listened with keen interest, and even Whittle, who did not know him well, could see that Talking Rock was disturbed by the news.

Meanwhile, approximately two miles north of Whittle and the Cheyennes, Stick sat in contemplative stillness with his back against the rough base of a cedar tree. He'd been sitting this way for three hours and didn't care if his body was comfortable or not. What were a few aching muscles compared to his sorrowful soul? Never mind his body. It would be there when he needed it to take the actions he was currently formulating in his mind.

Poor Stick was utterly torn with emotion. It was his fault that Whittle was dead. He should have left the boy in Wichita City. *No.* Stick bristled with anger. The fault lay at Pascuali Leon's feet. He was the man who would pay . . . just as soon as Stick located the canyon and figured out how to tackle a half-dozen fortified bandits. The will was there, if not the way.

Mercy and Ben, sensing Stick's anguish, watched silently over him throughout the night. Time-wise, it was not a long night, for dawn was bringing the summer solstice and the hours of darkness were diminished by the lengthened day. This year (as it happened) the solstice would be highlighted by a rising full moon. Although Stick was aware of the astronomical coincidence, it barely registered in the text of his ruminations. He dwelt on the pain of losing Whittle and on the desperate knowledge that only Evelyn Laroue could shed an ameliorative light on the void of that loss. The worth of Stick's whole life was on the line and he knew it. Nothing mattered now except Evelyn.

Stick thought and thought, and when the first pale hint

of sunshine appeared in the east, he shook the stiffness from his limbs and stood to meet the day. His first order of business was to feed oats to the horses, explaining patiently to both that he was going off without them and they should wait quietly for his return. He kissed Mercy on the nose before setting out on his second order of business, which was to locate and reconnoiter the canyon.

Talking Rock led Whittle and Brings the Rain north through the evergreen forest on a path that only he could see. They soon came to a break in the trees, where Talking Rock halted and pointed ahead. Whittle heeded the old man's direction and beheld Ben, who was relaxing in the shade with Mercy. Both horses were twitching their tails. Whittle's heart shot forward and his body followed.

When Ben saw Whittle coming, he temporarily forgot Stick's instructions to wait quietly in the forest and neighed excitedly. Even Mercy let down her guard and snorted gleefully.

While Whittle hugged his pony, Talking Rock walked to the cedar tree where Stick had sat through the night. On the ground were a coil of rope, a Winchester rifle, a saddle and a saddle pad. Talking Rock stepped past these items and reached up to take a black derby from between two branches. He tossed the hat to Whittle, who caught it and slapped it on his head in a single motion, then said brightly to Brings the Rain, "Stick must've known we were coming. That's good. I was afraid he thought I perished in the twister. I suspect that's what happened to Miss Prescott."

"Miss Prescott?" wondered Brings the Rain.

"Our packhorse," said Whittle. "Poor thing."

Stick felt hugely conspicuous as he walked north from the forest. There was nowhere to hide on the open plains and he feared discovery. Although he realized he would have been equally obvious on Mercy, he longed to go back and get her — at least then he could beat a rapid retreat and stand a fighting chance if he was attacked. However, he resisted the urge to fetch Mercy and continued cautiously ahead. Stealth was imperative at this stage of the hunt. His telescope was tucked in the back of his pants, his bowie knife was strapped to his left leg and his Sharps Fifty Caliber was in his right hand.

At mid-morning he found the first hill. It was an elongated hump lying west to east and ending in a gentle bluff on the plain. Stick circled around the bluff and turned west into a flat region between the first hill and the second. He trusted now that Only Olson had given him honest instructions. Even so, it took a lot of nerve for him to continue crossing the range.

There were seven hills altogether, the northernmost being the tallest and the steepest. Stick noticed something strange about the dry defile between the sixth and the seventh hills: At least twenty-five tumbleweeds were clumped together in what appeared to be a thistle graveyard. Wind currents had evidently driven the rolling weeds into the closed pocket of land.

Stick slithered on his stomach to the summit of the seventh hill, removed his sombrero and peeked over the crest. He had no need to employ his telescope. Approximately one thousand yards to the north a brick-brown sandstone column rose from the plain like a tower. It was every inch of a hundred feet tall and was surrounded at its base by a boulder-strewn field. Beyond it lay the sought-after canyon.

For an hour Stick lay without moving and studied the butte. As far as he could determine, there wasn't a lookout posted on the south or east side of the stone monolith. However, it seemed likely to Stick that there was a lookout, and that the man was installed on a north facing of the butte where he could look down over the canyon entrance. That was where Stick would have placed a guard if he were in charge of protecting the hideout.

Stick remained motionless for another hour. He knew he had to eventually go forward, yet he was in no rush to execute the inevitable. The thousand yards of sun-baked prairie between him and the butte was a daunting distance and he wanted to be sure his approach was made safely, without detection. At the end of that second hour, he decided to wait until high afternoon before setting forth. At that time shadows would be falling on the southeast side of obstacles and the sun would be strongest in the eyes of anyone watching the plains.

A man will do anything for a love he believes in. Stick proved this by remaining motionless and flat on his stomach in the baking heat for six hours while waiting for the sun to drop below its zenith. The whole while he concentrated on the butte. Not once did he think of food or water.

In due course the sun began its descending arc and shadows began pooling on the southeast side of things. Stick was about to slip over the crest of the seventh hill when he was struck by the odd feeling that someone was on the slope beside him. He turned and saw Talking Rock. The old man squatted on his heels with his arms resting on his knees and appeared to have been ensconced for a considerable length of time. Credit to Stick: He stiffened slightly, yet did not exclaim or gasp. It made sense to find the old Cheyenne warrior in the region of Bear Creek and Stick accepted his presence with a respectful nod. Talking Rock (who by some magic blended in perfectly with the landscape) replied with a lifted eyebrow. Although it was a small gesture, Stick took it to mean that his luck wasn't going to be all bad on this longest day of the year. Somehow the old man seemed to know what Stick was doing in the area, and more significantly, seemed willing to assist Stick in his bold endeavor.

Talking Rock glanced at the butte, then eyed Stick with a look that said there was a better way of approaching the canyon. It was lot to say with a look, yet the idea was so clear in the old man's mind that Stick fully comprehended the message. Talking Rock saw that Stick understood and started down the slope without further ado. Stick followed with complete faith in his guide. Intuitively he knew that Talking Rock intended to swing around and scout the backside of the canyon. The rapport that had sprung up between them abolished the need for words.

The men slunk up the dry valley and crept over the barren landscape as quietly and swiftly as two lizards on their way to a bug festival. They hardly stirred dust as they went, and when the sun set on this long day, Stick and Talking Rock lay side by side on a rock precipice between two crags on the western lip of the hidden canyon. Their view was commanding, both of the strawberry-colored moon that appeared in the sky and of Pascuali Leon's nefarious redoubt.

Meanwhile, back in the evergreen forest, Brings the Rain and Whittle were waiting. They had been waiting most of the day and were now growing somewhat anxious. Anxious for them was not hysterical. After all, Brings the Rain was a Cheyenne Indian and Whittle had been educated on the streets of Chicago. Still, they were concerned and felt the need to convince themselves that all was well. Brings the Rain began by remarking, "I am sure Stick is safe with Grandfather. Talking Rock sees what many miss. He could track a mouse from here to the Nescutunga and back."

"That's amazing." Whittle was impressed, yet equally proud of Stick. "Then I reckon they're both safe. My partner may look slim, but that man is tougher than pig-hide boots. We had a little brouhaha back in Caldwell. Stick picked up a bear-sized man and threw him clean across a store."

"He must be strong. What's a brewhaheha?"

"Sort of a ruckus. Kind of a fight. By the way, when you took off my boots, did you find a little gun?"

"No."

"No matter. We've got the rifle. I wonder what Stick and Talking Rock are doing now. Night is coming."

"Night is here."

"Hmmm. Yeah. Can Talking Rock really track a mouse?"

"I speak the truth."

"Wow. The best I can track is a cow."

SEVENTEEN

THE SUN FINISHED falling from the sky and a bright, all-but-full moon appeared. Stick and Talking Rock were watching the north face of the butte where a rifle-wielding bandit was in the act of descending. Crude ladders set up at difficult passages assisted the man's return to the canyon floor. Stick and Talking Rock keenly noted that no one ascended to replace the lookout. Evidently, the butte was only manned during daylight hours.

Stick almost bit a hole through his bottom lip when Evelyn Laroue and Adeline DeJarnette emerged from the smaller of two ramshackle huts in the canyon and walked to a spring between the hut and a corral containing nine horses. A man leaning against the corral gate also watched the hostages, but kept his distance and said nothing as Evelyn and Adeline washed their hands and faces. Perhaps this was because a woman with a shotgun stood in the doorway of the second, larger hut, watching both the man and the hostages. The woman was tall, solidly built, and had a wild, feral sort of sparkle in her cold blue eyes. Even so, she was not without a degree of feminine attractiveness and Stick presumed he was looking at Sadie Culpepper. Stick knew the identity of the bandit by the corral gate. He recognized the man's ugly face and the Colt .45 Peacemaker in his belt. It was the cretin named Curtis from Caldwell.

Stick turned his telescope to Evelyn, who, despite the dusty wear and tear of the circumstances that held her, looked the same as he remembered . . . if not more beautiful. Stick thought his heart would break. He could see that Evelyn was putting on a brave face for the young girl at her side. He wanted to stand up and yell out assurances to Evelyn and the girl. He did not. Instead he bit his bottom lip until he tasted blood.

During the next hour as Talking Rock and Stick studied the hideout they saw no sign of Pascuali Leon. Perhaps he was ensconced in the larger hut, or maybe he was not in the canyon. Pascuali's whereabouts hardly mattered — not to Stick, who counted six armed men, plus Sadie Culpepper, defending the captives. With odds like that, what difference would one more nemesis make?

After seeing all they needed to see, Stick and Talking Rock withdrew from their hiding position and Talking Rock led Stick along the outer rim of the canyon to the south side of the butte. Knowing the lookout had abandoned his post for the night, they stood openly amongst the boulders on the plain and studied the imposing monolith. Soon Talking Rock held a hand approximately four feet off the ground, pointed to himself, pointed to the moonlit tower, motioned at the ground and frowned. Instinctively, Stick understood that Talking Rock had climbed the butte as a boy and had a bit of trouble coming down.

Stick was not unduly surprised as Talking Rock led him directly toward the section of evergreen forest where Stick had left Mercy and Ben with his gear. Stick figured the old Indian had found the spot earlier, and that was how he'd known to seek out Stick in the first place. It seemed a reasonable explanation to Stick — not that he questioned Talking Rock's motives or needed any further validation of the man's helpful intentions.

Stick was in no way prepared for the shock he received when they returned to his bivouac in the forest. Of course, Stick thought Whittle was dead, so there was a good reason for his sudden loss of mental equilibrium.

Whittle sprang to his feet and spoke before Stick finished gasping. "There you are," the boy chirped happily.

Stick swallowed a porcupine.

The boy threw back his head and laughed. "I have to admit, Stick, I was worried about you."

"You were worried?" Stick responded incredulously. "The last I saw you, you were a hundred feet high, going sideways at two hundred miles an hour."

Whittle grinned and moved to hug Stick. "I said we'd find Bear Creek — even if it took flying."

"Dang," Stick muttered. He was too excited to express himself more articulately. Between seeing Evelyn, the tug of the waxing moon and Whittle's fond embrace, Stick felt a sudden surge of reckless optimism. There was a lot to do, but maybe — just maybe — they'd all get lucky and live.

The group soon put their feelings aside and concentrated on making a plan. It was only appropriate that Talking Rock should conduct the deliberations. He was the wisest person present and the one member of their council to have ever planned an assault on a defended position. Stick was pleased to defer. Where he had been a temporary soldier in a regimented army, Talking Rock had been a lifelong warrior in a struggle to protect his homeland. The old Indian arranged his eager assistants in a semicircle around him, borrowed Stick's bowie knife and began to etch the canyon's most prominent features in the dirt.

It went without saying that all their resources would be needed to conquer the odds and escape with the captives. To this end Talking Rock held no prejudices against the youngsters. The individual roles in the rescue attempt would be critical to its success. It was four against seven or eight. There were no tactical margins for soft sentiment.

Meanwhile, as the group hatched their plan, Evelyn Laroue huddled in the corner of a meanly functional hut stroking Adeline DeJarnette's long black hair. The eleven-year-old closely resembled her mother. Adeline was bright and naturally sweet-natured, yet her character had never been toughened by hardship and she was wholly dependent on her governess for emotional stability. Where Evelyn derived her own fortitude, she herself did not know — it simply existed for her to draw upon and she employed it without question. Her primary concern in the present circumstances was the child's fate. As for Evelyn's personal prospects, she was acquiescent. If the Good Lord meant to take her away as he took her mother's mind, her father's soul and the life of her true love, Melvin Fitchett, then throw open the Pearly Gates — she was ready to go.

"Evelyn?"

"Yes, Adeline?"

"Do you think Father forgot us?"

"No. It would be impossible for him to forget. I'm sure he is working on getting us out now."

"Father is stubborn sometimes. I hope help comes soon."

"It will."

"Maybe Father hired Wild Bill Hickok to fetch us. I heard he was looking for work."

"Adeline, let's not fret over who is coming. It's our job to be courageous and wait."

Brings the Rain translated as Talking Rock presented his plan, and as Stick listened, the burden of responsibility he felt for involving the others in the rescue mission turned to guilt. Talking Rock was sending the lambs into the wolf's den. According to his plan, sometime in the wee hours of the moonlit night the girl and the boy would descend a knotted rope hung from the precipice on the western lip of the canyon and penetrate the criminal camp. Once inside, they were to perform separate duties. While Whittle opened the corral gate and drove the horses through the narrow exit, Brings the Rain was to approach the smaller hut, alert the captives that help had arrived and guide them to the knotted rope, which they would climb and pull up behind them. As this was happening, Stick was to stand on the northern rim of canyon above the larger hut and distract the bandits with rifle fire. He would use the Sharps rifle. Talking Rock, who intended to climb the butte after the lookout descended, would employ one of the two Winchester rifles to cover Whittle and prevent any attempts at pursuit.

Stick tried to think positively, but it seemed to him the

youngsters were being sent on a suicide mission. In a best-case scenario, the girl and boy stood a forty-sixty chance of escaping unscathed. In the worst case, they would be unceremoniously shot. Stick's admiration for Talking Rock notwithstanding, he chose to differ with the man. "Hmph," Stick cleared his throat and caught Brings the Rain's attention. "Tell your grandfather that his plan is unsuitable. It asks too much of you and Whittle."

Brings the Rain gave Stick an affronted look before turning and translating for Talking Rock. She was obviously chagrined to hear her grandfather corrected. The old man listened patiently, then stared at the drawing in the dirt for several minutes. When he afterwards lifted his eyes to Stick, his thoughts needed no interpreter. Talking Rock believed his plan offered the only chance of success. Every element in the plan was imperative.

An awkward silence ensued. It was ended by Whittle, who addressed his partner directly. "We should do what Talking Rock says. I'm not afraid of going into the canyon."

It occurred to Stick that Whittle wished to impress Brings the Rain with his bravery, and saw it as his duty to dissuade the boy from an irrational commitment he would later regret. Stick told him forcefully, "You've never been shot at, Whittle, but take it from me, bullets do more than bite. If you go into that canyon, you may not be coming out."

Whittle replied with sudden passion. "I'm going into the canyon and spooking the horses. I won't be doing it for you, or Evelyn, or the DeJarnettes' little girl, or the money. I'm doing it because I owe the world a favor."

"You don't owe the world your life."

He thought otherwise. "Stick, as one Melvin to another, there's something I should tell you. I ought to have told you earlier."

"What?"

"Remember back when we met and you asked about Chicago burning down?"

Stick nodded. He remembered.

Whittle explained. Or rather, he confessed. "I started the fire that burned Chicago down. Slender Thomas and I were camping in a barn we knew about with lots of comfortable hay. We had a lantern lit and Slender Thomas asked me to extinguish the flame. I reached over my shoulder and accidentally knocked the lantern over. Kerosene spilled on the hay and caught fire quicker than you can say 'Get along, Mercy.' "

Stick gaped at Whittle with a mixture of disbelief and good old-fashioned awe. The boy was unique, that was certain, and Stick would not make the mistake of underestimating him again. Stick gradually collected his wits and asked, "What did you do?"

Whittle answered plainly, "I spent five minutes fighting the flame. It was no use. Then I helped Slender Thomas from the barn and looked around for help. We saw an Irish man with a wooden leg, hobbling up the street screaming 'Fire!' He must have smelled smoke or seen a flame. Anyway, Slender Thomas reckoned there was no need for two people to raise the alarm and recommended we make tracks for the Randolph Street Bridge. That's what we did. The rest of what I told you is true."

After quick consideration, Stick advised Whittle, "Don't blame yourself. Like you said, it was an accident."

"Yes, but a careless one that could have been avoided," the boy countered guiltily. "Anyhow, I'm just telling you I got reasons for what I need to do . . . and I won't feel better about myself until I balance the bad out with good."

Stick did not know what to say. There was a philosophical logic in his partner's way of thinking.

A sudden grin formed on Whittle's face. "Stick, something I've noticed about you. When you get troubled, you forget the bright side of things. Relax. A little luck and we'll all get out of there safely."

Luck, thought Stick. *When tomorrow night comes we're going to need a lot more than a little of that.*

During the whole of the above conversation Brings the Rain and Talking Rock listened politely without speaking or making any impatient facial gestures. Stick appreciated their tactful reserve, and now that matters were more or less settled between him and Whittle, he lowered his head to Talking Rock and said with a look that he was honored to join forces with the man and withdrew his previous objections. The old warrior understood and did not judge Stick harshly. He knew that armed conflicts came with bloody consequences and demanded fair debate for those involved.

The irony, of course, was that Stick harbored doubts while those who freely offered to help suffered no qualms — especially Talking Rock, who had no intentions of coming down from the butte alive. And yet, perhaps the trio's willingness to assist Stick was not ironic. Perhaps their fearless resolve existed simply as a component of the human condition and was a case of good people wishing to defeat the bad.

Stick fed the horses and handed out strips of beef jerky. The group sat in a circle and silently munched their food, then Talking Rock stood, spoke to Brings the Rain and slipped away into the forest. She watched him depart, turned slowly to face Stick and Whittle, shed a solitary tear that skidded down her left cheek and splattered on the ground, and said, "Grandfather has gone to prepare himself."

Whittle's heart ached as though it were squeezed in a

vise. He'd never seen or imagined a being more dear than Brings the Rain. The boy knew that Talking Rock was getting ready to sing his Death-song . . . and that his granddaughter would soon be alone in the world without a protector.

"We should rest," Stick said after a short while. He got up, retrieved his bedroll from under the cedar tree and unfurled it on the ground beside Brings the Rain. "Use this," he told her tenderly before returning to the tree and sitting with his back against the trunk. He had a lot of hard thinking to do.

So did Whittle.

So did Brings the Rain.

Only Talking Rock's mind was free of care.

EIGHTEEN

MELVIN FITCHETT WAS sitting on a cot in a crowded ward of a Confederate Army hospital when a uniformed captain appeared in the doorway and pointed to him. Melvin stood and saluted. The officer said in a commanding tone, "General Lee wishes to see you in his tent." As Melvin followed the captain he could feel the curious stares of his fellow wounded. No one seemed to think it odd when Melvin and the captain passed through the hospital walls. They crossed a lawn toward a white tent and the captain suddenly disappeared. A voice from within the tent bid Melvin to enter. He did so and saw Robert E. Lee. The great man stood with his hands behind his back and his eyes glowed like burning coals. Distant bugles sounded a battle charge and then Lee said, "We have given much. Remember the rolling fire." Melvin looked down. He'd lost his voice.

Stick lifted his gaze and saw Talking Rock standing before him with his face streaked in horizontal red and yellow lines. The feather had been taken from the old man's hair and hung on a string around his neck. He was ready for war.

Talking Rock signalled to Brings the Rain, who went to his side, and after he spoke, she translated for Stick, "Grandfather wonders if you have words from your chief?"

Stick stood and shook the sleep from his limbs. It took him a moment to understand what Talking Rock was asking. Suddenly he did, and answered. "My chief says, 'We have given much. Remember the rolling fire.'"

"What is rolling fire?"

Stick didn't know. Did Lee speak of the fire at Wilderness? He'd appeared there in a previous dream. But no. The Wilderness fire had swept through the trees — not rolled. Whittle joined the group and Stick wondered: *Did Lee know about the Chicago fire? Had it rolled from house to house?*

Whittle could see from everyone's expression that they were considering some important matter and he asked generally, "What?"

"Do you know the rolling fire?" replied Brings the Rain. When Whittle failed to answer, she added, "What does it mean?"

"You know, spinning," said Whittle, making a quick motion with his hands. "Turning over . . . like pigweed in the wind."

Something clicked in Stick. "That's it!" He turned excitedly to Talking Rock and said through Brings the Rain, "The tumbleweed graveyard between the sixth and seventh hills. I can light several on fire and roll them down the wall of the canyon against the rear of the big hut. That will make for a distraction. I've got store-bought matches in my saddlebag. Been carrying them since Texas."

When Brings the Rain translated Stick's words for Talking Rock, the old man's face lit with approval and he said with a look that he admired Stick's craftiness. Stick was humbled. He'd been elevated a notch in Talking Rock's eyes. The old man grunted, tapped Stick's chest with a bony finger and the RollingFireTumbleweed proposal was thereupon adopted. They later decided to use the rolling fire as a signal for springing into action. Stick would wait until the two youths were in position before igniting the first tumbleweed. When they saw the flaming ball on the canyon slope, Brings the Rain would lead the captives from the hut to the knotted rope and Whittle would break loose with the horses. Stick would roll down a second tumbleweed, then start shooting at whoever ran from the hut. Talking Rock would join in the melee when he determined the moment was ripe.

That was the plan. However, as anyone who has ever devised a complicated tactical assault knows, the prescribed events are often altered by variables on the ground.

Evelyn Laroue awoke with a crick in her neck, a cramp in one leg and a bruised left shoulder. The bruise was from attempting to crash through a door an hour after she and Adeline were snatched off the street. Evelyn also had a scratch across the bridge of her nose. That came after she slapped Sadie Culpepper, and Sadie Culpepper slapped her back. These physical woes aside, Evelyn's mental state was fine. She wasn't cheerful or giddily optimistic, but her outlook was steady and there remained room in her heart for hope. Thank goodness for that, for Evelyn had ultimately resigned herself to hope throughout the past ten days and nights of captivity. Or was it twelve? Somewhere along the line Evelyn had lost count. It hardly mattered. She was wisely responding to her situation one hour at a time.

This morning, at this hour, as Evelyn cradled Florence and Rolland DeJarnette's daughter in her arms and scanned the dingy confines, she experienced an itchy feeling that things were about to change. Call it a subtle premonition. Call it hope keeping pace with heightened desperation. Evelyn sensed change, and change, under current circumstances, would almost have to be good.

Not so many miles south of the derelict hut where Evelyn was experiencing her itchy feeling, Stick and Whittle were sitting in a patch of sunlight on the forest floor. Stick was busy tying a sequence of double knots in the coil of rope at his feet. Whittle was idly watching. Twenty yards away, Talking Rock was informing Ben and Mercy of their role in the upcoming getaway. They were to go with him to the south base of the butte and wait secretively amongst the boulders for Whittle or Stick to appear with further instructions. The horses easily understood their assignment and nodded simultaneously. Both were eager to please Talking Rock. A short distance beyond Talking Rock and the horses, Brings the Rain lay on her back peering at a clear blue sky. Now and then she threw a furtive glance at Whittle. There was something about him that caused her to consider the future.

After Stick tested the tenth and final knot at the end of the rope, he told Whittle, "We'll anchor this before I move into position. The overhang where you're going down cuts away sharply. You won't have any rock to brace your feet against. You go first and hold it steady for Brings the Rain."

"That's the best way," agreed Whittle.

"The walls are thirty feet steep on that side of the canyon, and that's why Leon doesn't have it watched closely, so if you go slowly and don't make any noises you're not likely to be seen. Anyway, how do you plan to carry your rifle?"

Whittle grimaced. "I hadn't thought of that. What do you advise?"

"On your back. I'll make you a strap that's easy to unhook."

"Thanks, Stick. You're mighty helpful."

"Me? You're volunteering to risk your life for people you don't even know."

Whittle shrugged. "We discussed that before. It's nothing."

Stick's expression indicated differently. "See it however you want, Whittle, but I'll always owe you a favor."

"I'll take you up on one now."

"Name it."

"Whether I live or die down in the canyon, and especially if I die, don't tell anybody what I told you about Chicago."

"I won't."

"Thanks. How about you, you want a favor?"

"Naw. Just wish me luck, that's all."

Although the day was filled with many hard-boiled thoughts and long moments, the hours ticked past and it eventually ended with the sun setting in the west. Afterwards a fully illuminated moon made a seemingly magical debut in a lower quadrant of the southeast sky. Talking Rock looked at the moon, then looked at Stick, who looked at Whittle, who looked at Brings the Rain, and thus everyone present knew it was time to leave. Ben swished his tail and neighed to Mercy. She stamped a foot and whinnied in horse-tongue: "Yes, Ben, I know we are going with

Talking Rock. Now don't get ahead of yourself. Wait for his command."

They started out in single file, with Stick on point and Talking Rock in the rear with the horses. They had not gone very far before Whittle noticed that Brings the Rain walked without making a sound. Nothing. Nary a crunch or a squeak. Any twig she stepped upon crumbled instead of snapping, and if she dislodged a pebble, it flipped over silently and lay on its side. Whittle was amazed and made a brief attempt to imitate her movements, yet he soon abandoned the effort. For the first time since putting them on in Caldwell, he perceived a drawback to the new boots he'd been so proudly wearing. *Oh, well,* he reasoned. *I'm armed with a rifle. I can afford to make more noise than Brings the Rain. It would be better if we were invisible.*

The group passed cautiously around the eastern bluffs of the first six hills and entered the divide south of the seventh. It was almost midnight and the moon was at its brightest. Once beyond the brunt of the hill they all paused. This was where Brings the Rain, Whittle and Stick would take their leave of Talking Rock, who was staying behind with the horses. It was a solemn occasion, thick with sentiment — yet, because Brings the Rain and Talking Rock would not let it be so, the parting was not terribly sad. The girl knew she would never see her grandfather living again, and yet she was also aware that he was going to greet the Great Maker, and for that she was joyful. Talking Rock lay down the rifle he was carrying and wrapped his arms around Brings the Rain. They stood this way for a minute, then he released her and faced Whittle. When the boy doffed his derby and bowed, Talking Rock placed the palms of his hands together and inclined his head. Then the old man whirled around, poked Stick's chest with a finger and softly clicked his tongue. It was his way of saying good luck. Promptly thereafter, Brings the Rain, Whittle and Stick started toward the west end of the narrow valley.

When they reached the tumbleweed graveyard Brings the Rain and Whittle waited off to one side while Stick took stock of the available selections. He soon picked a smaller, compact thistle and inserted it into a bigger, hollow tumbleweed. Then he crammed the whole affair into an even larger orb, which he held out and checked for heft. Pleased with his creation, he repeated the process. When the second ball was ready he withdrew twine that he had cut for the purpose, snatched the orbs together, tossed them over his left shoulder and returned to his companions.

There is no apt analogy for the image Stick projected as he emerged from the tumbleweed graveyard. To properly conceive the picture one must first imagine a tall, slender man wearing a sombrero silhouetted in the moonlight between two translucent spheres and a coil of rope. Add to this a purposeful stride and the hard line of a rifle, and one only begins to approximate the impression Brings the Rain and Whittle received of Stick coming toward them.

Stick guided the youngsters west from the hills, swooped around to the north, turned east and led them directly toward the flat rock situated between the two crags on the west end of the canyon. As they neared the precipice Stick halted and hooked the tumbleweeds to a tuft of grass growing near the foot of the steep slope. Then he ushered Brings the Rain and Whittle up the path Talking Rock had shown him. Soon the climbers reached their goal and peered out over the canyon.

Stick found a solid slab of stone projecting from the northern crag and fastidiously secured the unworked end of the rope to the slab. While he was doing so, Brings the Rain and Whittle were surveying the geography below, orienting themselves with respect to their individual assignments. When Stick came forward and cautiously lowered the knotted end of the rope into the canyon he was not wrong in thinking: *Brings the Rain and Whittle form a fearless pair.*

Minutes later Stick was at the base of the outer canyon wall retrieving the tumbleweeds he had left there. He slung the near-weightless orbs over his shoulder and paused for an instant to view the brightly luminescent moon. Unbeknownst to him, at this precise moment, Evelyn Laroue was peering through a crack in the hut roof, also viewing the moon. Earlier in the day she had been convinced that change was in the air and that the ugly circumstances that gripped her were about to improve. But nothing had happened, and now she was feeling angry and let down. She wanted to scream and run from the hut, which was unlocked and unguarded, yet there was no egress from the canyon other than the protected passage beyond the corral and the main hut where Pascuali Leon lingered, and she knew she'd never make it there without detection. An attempt to do so would only invite derision from her captors and Evelyn refused to provide them with a reason to ridicule her more than they already had. She gritted her teeth and concentrated on the moon. She would not give in to despair — not while Adeline DeJarnette needed her strength, not while there was air in her lungs, not while she had hope in her heart.

NINETEEN

STICK HAD EVERYTHING set around him. His breech-loading Sharps rifle was on his right and two dozen fifty-caliber bullets were stacked nearby. A little behind him and to his left rested the tumbleweeds. Moments before he had installed an arrangement of stick matches in the center of both orbs; they would serve as both fuse and accelerant. In his right hand he held additional matches. He had already picked out a rock on which to strike the first match. All he had to do now was act.

Stick waited. He wanted to give his team extra minutes to get in position. He worried about Talking Rock. How anyone, much less an old man, could negotiate the sheer south side of the butte at night, he could not readily fathom. Yet Talking Rock had set out to do so . . . and Stick had to presume his success.

Talking Rock had gained the summit, yet in the course of his ascent he'd been compelled to wedge the Winchester rifle in a crevice to use as prop for climbing. Afterwards, the daring old man had been unable to reach down and dislodge the weapon. He now stood alone on the lofty peak, armed only with his wisdom and sacrificial will.

Evelyn tensed and looked around her. Although Adeline was
asleep on the floor beside her, she could have sworn she heard
a girl whisper her name. An instant later she heard the voice
again. "Eveleen," it called softly through the door. Evelyn
sprang to her feet and tiptoed across the hut. "I am a friend of
Stick and Whittle," the voice said softly. Evelyn searched her
mind. She had no idea who Stick or Whittle might be, yet the
voice sounded trustworthy, so she drew open the door. Brings
the Rain stepped inside and whispered, "Hello. We are going
from this place with the rolling fire. Take off your shoes."

Evelyn was confused. "Excuse me?"

"We are going from this place."

"When?"

"Soon."

"How?"

"Up a rope that waits. Wake the girl."

"Who are you?"

"Brings the Rain."

"God bless you for coming."

"Hurry now." Brings the Rain moved into the doorway.
"I am watching for fire."

Two burly bandits snoozed back-to-back near the rail gate of
the makeshift corral as Whittle snaked forward on his stom-

ach. Lacking Brings the Rain's perfect silence, Whittle was pretending he was invisible. So far the ruse seemed to be working. Except for a large bay stallion that watched his every move, no one suspected his presence. Whittle inched his way to the south side of the crude pen, squatted low on his heels and began waiting for the signal. His grip on the Winchester was fierce. He was not afraid, exactly, yet his arms and legs trembled, and he was ready to explode with excitement. Despite asserting otherwise to Stick, his participation in the rescue effort had nothing to do with Chicago. Whittle was not making amends with the past. He was here for his partner, who had accepted him when he needed acceptance and earned his eternal friendship. He was also here for Brings the Rain, who made him aware of feelings he had never known existed.

Suddenly Whittle cringed. The stallion had moved to his side of the corral and was glaring suspiciously at him. Whittle's best hope was that the creature smelled Ben and Mercy on his clothes and was merely curious about the strange scent. It was partially the case. Unfortunately the stallion also sensed that Whittle was an intruder and opted to warn the other horses. It reared onto its hind legs, snorted violently and pounded its front hooves onto the rail above Whittle's head. This roused the men by the gate. The swiftest of the pair popped to his feet, yanked a pistol from his belt and trained it on the boy. Stick had warned Whittle that the men from the Beale brothers' store were members of Leon's gang, and Whittle immediately recognized the vermin named Curtis. In a flash — before the man could shoot him — Whittle lifted the Winchester rifle and shot the Colt pistol from the man's hand. As the shot rang out, the horses began to mill about nervously in the pen and the second man darted around the corral toward the shooter. Whittle did not hesitate. He jumped in amongst the stirred-up animals and started working his way toward the gate. He was thinking: *Come on, Stick. Roll the fire.*

Stick heard the shot as he was in the act of striking the first match. Startled by the sound, he snapped the stick match in half without drawing a spark. Frantically, he repeated the effort. Fire appeared and he thrust it into the desiccated guts of a waiting tumbleweed. The trigger-matches erupted as planned and a flame was established. Stick promptly hoisted the burning sphere over his head and hurled it into the canyon.

Brings the Rain turned and whispered sharply. "There's the fire. Let's run."

Evelyn grabbed Adeline by the arm and moved forward. "Go. We're right behind you."

The threesome burst from the shack as fast as their legs would carry them.

Whittle was at the gate when he saw the rolling fire. At the same time Curtis saw him. The outlaw had recovered somewhat from the numbing shock to his right hand and now wielded the menacing Colt in his left. Whittle threw open the gate and scuttled back into the throng of agitated horses. He had temporarily lost sight of the second man, but then a shot rang out and his derby flew from his head. So much for the hat. Whittle now knew exactly where his attacker stood. He whirled about and — not having the heart to shoot the man in the chest — shot him in the shoulder. Whittle wasted no time cocking the Winchester and rotating toward the gate where Curtis was looming. As Whittle spun around he saw a flash of light in the corner of his eye. Curtis obviously saw it too, for he froze and watched in awe as an orange ball of fire rolled down the canyon side, bounced from a rock, skipped across the roof of the main hut, bounced again on the canyon floor, then soared over the fence into the corral. Spewing sparks spooked the already anxious horses and sent them stampeding through the open gate. The ugly man named Curtis was in the wrong spot at the wrong time. He was knocked on his backside and trampled.

Stick had the second tumbleweed lit before the first shattered and burnt out in the corral. He tossed this one less forcefully than the first and bent to pick up his rifle. Three shots had already been fired and he knew someone was in trouble. He could not see, but he figured it was Whittle. Stick was unable to imagine anyone taking a shot at Evelyn, or Brings the Rain, or the DeJarnettes' little girl.

"Quick. Go," barked Brings the Rain. "Someone is coming."

"Pull, Adeline. PULL UP."

"I'm pulling."

"Harder. I'm with you."

"You must hurry."

Whittle followed the horses from the corral, jumped over the pummeled man by the gate and ran a dozen feet before halting. Sadie Culpepper and Pascuali Leon had charged from the hut in front of him and both were bearing rifles. A frightening pair. It struck Whittle that he was looking at a witch and a pirate. A stream of spite spewed from the woman's eyes and a twisted sort of hatred emanated from the man. In the next few seconds two things happened simultaneously. One: The woman took aim at Whittle with her rifle, and just as she did, he heard a pistol cock behind him. He had not finished dropping to the ground when both weapons reported. Two: Pascuali, seeing that Sadie had a bead on the intruder, turned toward the west of the canyon where a couple of his men were fleeing the action. Pascuali despised deserters, so he shot them one by one in the back.

Both sequences ended poorly for the bad guys. In the first: Sadie Culpepper and the man Whittle had previously wounded in the shoulder were each struck in a crossfire. The man pitched to the ground and died. Sadie sank slowly down and clutched her stomach. In the second: Two of Leon's men were killed before reaching the dangling rope at the west end of the canyon, and now neither was able to tell their boss that they'd seen the captives escape with an Indian girl.

Whittle didn't wait for Leon to recover from the shock of seeing Sadie's blood-stained stomach. He scampered after the horses toward the narrow exit at the east end of the canyon.

Stick was watching with one eye when Whittle ran into view from behind the hut. With his other eye, he was watching the two confused men standing near the mouth of the exit. "Where was Talking Rock?" Stick wondered. He wasn't allowed time to dwell on the matter, for suddenly one of the men pulled a pistol from his belt and pointed the barrel past the horses at the boy. Stick hated to do it, but he shot the scoundrel before the man could pull back on the trigger. Stick's shot was low and it came as some relief to him when the bandit grabbed his left leg and dove to the ground. When his cowardly sidekick wisely did the same, Stick shot over the man's head as a warning. The two men lay quivering in fear.

Whittle was some sixty or seventy yards from the exit when Leon whistled shrilly and the big bay stallion broke away from the pack of horses, reversed course and galloped back toward its master. One and a half seconds later Whittle and the stallion blew past each other, sprinting in opposite directions.

Whittle was twenty yards from the narrow passageway leading out of the canyon when he heard hooves thundering behind him. Pascuali Leon had mounted and was on his way.

Stick reached to snatch a bullet from his pile. *Grr.* He fumbled the bullet and wasted precious seconds loading his rifle. *Damn.* By the time he was ready to shoot at Leon, Whittle had advanced, and Stick had lost his angle of fire. However much Stick may have wished to stop Leon, he would not risk shooting the boy.

Whittle scrambled into the gap. Five heart-thumps later

Pascuali Leon and the stallion charged in behind him. Whittle's heart thumped again . . . then skipped a beat as a cry pierced the air above. It was a glorious, ululating cry. It was Talking Rock saying hello to his Creator as he swooped down from the sky.

Pascuali Leon never knew what hit him. He just crumbled into the rock wall where he was driven by the flying warrior.

TWENTY

"WELL, WE DID it!" Whittle triumphantly declared as he and Stick stood with the horses approximately one hundred yards east of the canyon.

"Yeah," Stick replied with half-hearted enthusiasm.

"Of course, it took a little luck, didn't it?"

Stick nodded.

Whittle's demeanor shifted from cheery to sad. "I never would have made it without Talking Rock. He saved my life. I aim to make it up to him by taking care of his granddaughter."

"That would be a good thing," Stick mumbled distractedly. He could see Brings the Rain coming over the ridge with Adeline and Evelyn.

Whittle followed Stick's line of sight, saw the approaching females, then looked askance at his partner and chuckled, "I know what's wrong with you. You're skittish."

"No I'm not," Stick grumbled.

Whittle threw back his head and laughed. "Yes you are. You're more skittish than that roadrunner we saw."

Stick furrowed his brow and allowed, "I might be a little jumpy."

Brings the Rain led Evelyn and Adeline over the north ridge of the canyon and guided them onto the plain. When Evelyn first saw the man and boy waiting with the horse and pony she did not recognize the man. She was expecting to meet strangers named Stick and Whittle.

Stick could not speak as the party approached. All he could do was gaze timidly at his long-lost sweetheart.

Evelyn drew in a sharp breath and nearly stumbled when she got a good look at the man standing with the boy. Her eyes were telling her something her mind could not fathom and her heart fluttered wildly with confusion. Could this be?! Was that the man she prayed for?

Stick removed his sombrero.

Evelyn's voice cracked with incredulity. "Melvin Fitchett?"

After Stick just stood there, Whittle jabbed him with an elbow and whispered, "Go kiss her."

Except for trembling, Melvin "Stick" Fitchett did not move.

Evelyn took one step forward. "Please speak. Let me hear your voice."

Stick swallowed. "Evelyn, it's me, Melvin. I was wounded at Wilderness, but I didn't die. I've been wanting to tell you that for a long — " Evelyn rushed forward and wrapped her arms around Melvin before he could complete his sentence. It didn't matter to him. Nothing mattered now except now.

As Evelyn clung to Melvin Fitchett and nestled her face against his shoulder and neck, she stammered, "I . . . my Lord . . . my prayers . . . somehow I knew. I never had the feeling you died and couldn't believe it. You're here. . . ."

All Stick could think to say was, "And you're here too."

Whittle winked at Brings the Rain and grinned. She allowed a quick smile to cross her face, then produced a worried look and nodded over her shoulder toward the canyon. Whittle immediately understood her concern. Surviving members of Leon's gang might be organizing a pursuit at this very moment. Whittle turned to Evelyn and Stick and coughed to get their attention. "Excuse me, but you two might want to save that for later. Right now, we ought to be going."

Stick smiled, and without disengaging from their embrace, informed Evelyn, "That's my partner, Whittle. He has an impatient nature."

"How do you do, Ma'am?"

"Fine, thank you," Evelyn answered giddily.

Stick turned his gaze to the little girl standing by Brings the Rain. "Hello. You must be Adeline. I promised your mother I'd bring you home."